PRAISE FOR
KRISTINE KATHRYN RUSCH

"Rusch is a great storyteller."

—*RT Book Reviews*

"Whether [Rusch] writes high fantasy, horror, sf, or contemporary fantasy, I've always been fascinated by her ability to tell a story with that enviable gift of invisible prose. She's one of those very few writers whose style takes me right into the story—the words and pages disappear as the characters and their story swallows me whole....Rusch has style."

—Charles de Lint

"A masterful writer is at work."

—Orson Scott Card

"Rusch's greatest strength…is her ability to close down a story and leave the reader feeling that the author could not possibly have wrung any more satisfaction out of the piece."

—*The Kansas City Star*

"Rusch is a great storyteller—easily the equal of Patterson or Koontz."

—*Analog*

"Kristine Kathryn Rusch is one of the best writers in the field."

—*SFRevu*

"[Rusch's] writing style is simple but elegant, and her characterization excellent."

—Mark Morris
Beyond

"Kristine Kathryn Rusch's crime stories are exceptional, both in plot and in style."

—Ed Gorman
Mystery Scene Magazines

Praise for the Retrieval Artist series

"If you love puzzle mysteries, crime novels, well-invented sci-fi worlds, or stories about characters you can believe in and care about, you owe it to yourself to give Rusch's Retrieval Artist novels a try."

—Orson Scott Card
New York Times bestselling author

"What links [Miles Flint] to his most memorable literary ancestors is his hard-won ability to perceive the complex nature of morality and live with the burden of his own inevitable failure."

—*Locus*

Praise for the Smokey Dalton series
(writing as Kris Nelscott)

"Nelscott's series setting, in the turbulent late '60s, gives her books layers of issues of racism, class, and war, all of which still seem to remain sadly timely today."
—*Oregonian*

"Nelscott has her own, very distinct voice, and her series creates its own deeply satisfying pleasures and cogent points."
—*Seattle Times*

"Nelscott is good at conveying the edgy caution that blacks once brought to their movements among white society."
—*Houston Chronicle*

"(A) crime writer deliberately taking chances."
—*Chicago Tribune*

"It's not hard to draw parallels between Nelscott's PI Smokey Dalton and Walter Mosley's Easy Rawlins, another secretive, canny black man trying to solve mysteries while circumspectly navigating the white world. But Dalton's no knock-off. (Would you label the hundreds of hard-boiled detectives who've appeared in Raymond Chandler's wake mere Marlow Xeroxes because they're white?)"
—*Entertainment Weekly*

Five Oregon Stories
Kristine Kathryn Rusch

WMG
Publishing

Five Oregon Stories

Copyright © 2013 Kristine Kathryn Rusch
Published 2013 by WMG Publishing
www.wmgpublishing.com
Cover art copyright © Jpldesigns/Dreamstime
Book and cover design copyright © 2013
by WMG Publishing
Cover design by Allyson Longueira/WMG Publishing
ISBN-13: 978-0-615-75880-0
ISBN-10: 0-615-75880-0

"The One That Got Away" by Kristine Kathryn Rusch first published in The UFO Files, edited by Martin H. Greenberg and Ed Gorman, Daw Books, 1998.

"Going Native" by Kristine Kathryn Rusch first published in Amazing Stories, Fall, 1998.

"The Amazing Quizmo" by Kristine Kathryn Rusch first published in The North American Review, May-August, 2009.

"Patriotic Gestures" by Kristine Kathryn Rusch first published in Scene of The Crime, edited by Dana Stabenow, Running Press, 2008.

"The Moorhead House" by Kristine Kathryn Rusch first published in Ellery Queen's Mystery Magazine, January, 2008.

WMG Publishing
www.wmgpublishing.com

Contents

Five Oregon Stories
Kristine Kathryn Rusch

Introduction

I THINK OF MYSELF AS A MIDWESTERN NATIVE, even though I am not. I was born in New York State. I have now lived in Oregon longer than I have lived anywhere else. I often joke that my entire life's saga has been about moving west until I ran out of land. In 1995, I moved to the Oregon Coast. The Pacific Ocean is across the highway from my house.

I call myself a Midwestern native because my family lives there. My parents, grandparents, siblings, nieces and nephews were all born there. The older generations are buried there, and the younger generations populate Wisconsin, Minnesota, Iowa, Indiana, and North Dakota.

As rooted as I am in the Midwest, I am really not a Midwesterner any longer. I'm not polite. I don't say "you're welcome" after someone thanks me. I grunt in acknowledgement, the way that Pacific Northwesterners do. I dress down even when I'm supposed to dress up. I like mild weather. I hate mosquitoes.

I also love this state. Oregon is unusual in a variety of ways. We are a northern state, but our weather is, for the most part, mild. In the western part of the state, snow is a phenomenon.

We have mountains, forests, rivers, lakes, desert, and something called a Gorge. It's a cut through the northern part of the state that allows the Columbia River to flow through it, and it has a weather system all its own.

In fact, it takes the weather announcers eight to ten minutes of the newscast to predict the state's weather, because we have so many different climates. It might be snowing on top of Mt. Hood, but raining in the Willamette Valley and sunny on the Oregon Coast.

Our government is equally strange. Our legislature meets once every two years, whether we need it or not. When I moved to the state, no mayor got a salary except for the mayor of Portland. The rest "volunteered" their time. If you want to defeat a candidate or a ballot measure, prove that their funding comes from out of state.

When I moved here, the semi-official motto of Oregon was "Welcome to Oregon. Now leave." It's not semi-official any more, but it is still a motto. Those of us who stay eventually stop feeling like outsiders. We know we're part of the community when we start complaining about the "foreigners"—and by that, we don't mean people from other countries. We mean people from other states.

As you can tell, Oregon has seeped into this Midwesterner's soul. So I write about the state regularly. The stories in this collection are all set in Oregon for a reason. I needed something particularly Oregon in order to tell the story.

In "The One That Got Away," I needed a casino that tolerates strange locals. So I placed Spirit Winds in a town that doubles for many of the coastal towns, the fictional Seavy Village. (I've written other stories and novels set there.) I know coastal casinos tolerate strange locals because I live on the coast, and the only thing that keeps our casino in business in the winter is—you guessed it—strange locals.

"Going Native," is about a fictional national experience, but the crazies that my journalist visits have their convention in Eastern Oregon—because lots of wacky people gather up there, primarily for the privacy that the crazy TVSo?s would want.

"The Amazing Quizmo" takes place in Portland, the state's largest city. Portland has bike messengers, an active bar trivia community, and lots of underemployed smart people. I suppose I could have set it in New York City, but New York is too big for the quizmaster to know everyone who frequents trivia quizzes.

"Patriotic Gestures" happens in a made-up bedroom community of Portland—a place that once had its own identity but is slowly being swallowed by the folks from the big city. You'll see why such a place is essential to the story.

Finally, "The Moorhead House" takes place in another fictional Oregon community, this one in Oregon's Willamette Valley. The liberal valley has the largest population in the state. Oregon's three largest cities are within two hours of each other down the I-5 corridor. "The Moorhead House" takes elements of all three cities and makes a new city, but one with a very Oregon flavor.

I hope you enjoy the stories set in my adopted home state. If you do, keep an eye out for more stories from Oregon. I'll have another short collection of Oregon stories relatively soon. I have no idea how many Oregon stories I've written, but I know it's a lot.

—Kristine Kathryn Rusch
Lincoln City, Oregon
July 12, 2010

The One That Got Away

*I*T HAPPENED AT THE THURSDAY NIGHT blackjack tournament, and we were miffed. Not because it happened, but because of *when* it happened. And to get to that will take a bit of explaining, both about the tournament and about us.

There are about ten of us, and we call ourselves the Tuesday/Thursday regulars because we never miss a tournament. The local Native American casino—the Spirit Winds—held an open tournament every Tuesday and Thursday. Anyone could play if he put up twenty bucks, and if he won, he got a share of the pot. The pot consisted of the buy-in fees, and the buy-back fees plus another hundred added by the casino. The casino made no money on the tournament. The game was a freebie designed to get people into the casino—and it got me there twice a week.

Me, and nine others. There were more regulars than us, of course, but we were the ones who never skipped a week. I was a pretty good player—I'd made a living counting cards in the mid-seventies—and I'd swear that Tigo Jones had professional card-playing experience as well. Five more of the regulars played basic strategy, and the rest, well, they relied upon luck or God or their moods to supply their strategy. It worked for them every once in a while.

In blackjack, you learn to honor luck.

The good players just try to minimize it. They try to rely on skill. But luck can win out, in the end, if you're not careful.

On most nights, pot's only worth about two hundred to the winner, a hundred to second place, and fifty to third, with four dinner comps to sop the folks who made it to the final round. What that means is that there's good money in this for me and Tigo because we place every four tournaments we play. A few regulars are losing money each time they play, and about five—those basic strategy guys—are giving their gambling fund an occasional shot in the arm.

It's all in good fun, and we've become a family of sorts—the kind of family that barflies make or old ladies make when they work on church social after church social. We look after each other, and we gossip about each other, and we tolerate each other, whether we like each other or not.

We also know who's crazy and who isn't, and, except for Joey, the kid who is pissing his inheritance away twenty dollars at a time, no one who shows up for the blackjack tournaments at Spirit Winds is crazy.

Or, at least, that's what we hope.

***

THAT NIGHT, I NOTICED A FEW STRANGE things before I even made it to Spirit Winds. For one thing, the ocean was so black it was impossible to see. Now, the ocean is never black. It reflects light—and even if the sky is completely dark, the ocean isn't because it's reflecting the light of nearby homes. In fact, I like the ocean on cloudy nights because it has a luminescence all its own, a glow that makes it look alive from within.

The second strange thing was that there was no wind. None. Zero, zip, zilch. We usually have a breeze in Seavy Village and often have more than that. The ocean again. It is a major part of our lives.

And the final strange thing was the power outage that swept through the neighborhoods like anxious fingers pinching out candles. I didn't know about that until later—the casino has back up generators—and if I had known, well, it would have made no difference.

I would have been at the tournament anyway.

I have nothing better to do.

You see, I call myself retired, but really what I am is hiding out. I'm good enough to play in big tournaments, but when Spirit Winds holds its semi-annual $10,000 tournament, I'm conveniently out of town. That way, I don't have to fill out a 1099, and I don't have to show three pieces of i.d, and all the correct tax information. Because I don't have three valid pieces of i.d, and I haven't filed taxes since 1978, the year I fled Nevada with the wrong kind of folks at my heels. I moved too fast to get any fake i.d., and so I lived off cash for far too long. By the time I had settled down, I didn't know anybody in that business any more. The government had closed the loopholes making fake ids simple for anyone with half a brain, and I really didn't want to put fingers out to the criminal element, since it was the criminal element I'd been running from.

I confessed to a local banker with hippie sympathies, let him think I had been underground since my college activist days, and had him set me up a checking account. It's amazing what a man can do with a checking account—the lies he can tell to get him a real life in a small town.

But it couldn't get me a driver's license, nor could it get me a credit card. I still use cash much of the time, and a lot of that cash comes from my safety deposit box in the aforementioned bank. The gambling at the small casino is just incidental. I figure I'm old enough now that no one would recognize me and my problem is so out of date that the folks who were looking for me are either dead or in prison. But I have learned to be cautious by nature. I don't rub anyone the wrong way.

And I never, ever call attention to myself.

***

THE TOURNAMENT WAS BIG THAT NIGHT, bigger than it had ever been. Later I learned the reason: the power outage. The casino was packed on a Thursday because much of Seavy Village had lost their lights, their heat, and their cable. I had been in the casino since mid-afternoon. I'd been on a roll at one of the regular tables, parlaying my lucky hundred dollar chip into six thousand. Normally that puts you in tax declaration territory, but I would get five hundred on one table, then pocket it, and move to the next. I was hot that afternoon, and it felt good.

Lucky streaks are important. Knowing how to maximize them is even more important, and that's what I was doing. Perfecting the old skills.

When I reached six grand, my brain shut off, and I decided to replenish it with food. I had a solitary dinner at the buffet, and then wandered to the tournament tables.

There were a lot of unfamiliar faces around the table, and I was burdened with a small fortune in chips, stuck in my pockets and my fanny pack. I couldn't take anything to the car because I didn't have one, and I also didn't have time to walk home. I'd been in that situation before, and I'd learned not to be too friendly. The last time I'd told one of the regulars about my run and a pit boss overheard. I had to spend a good fifteen minutes making a show of losing the money at various tables.

Normally the pit bosses don't tell on me. They tolerate me and Tigo and the other local professionals. It's the out-of-towners they kick out of the casino. Oregonians and their dislike of "foreigners." Gotta love 'em.

That night, though, I wasn't taking any chances. I leaned against one of the slot machines and smoked a cigarette, adding to the thick, slightly bluish air already growing around the tables. The casino is new and modern,—no tokens for slots, only cash and cards—high ceilings, good traffic flow. The place feels more like a spa than a casino, especially the casinos of my heyday. I still miss the chink-chink of tokens as they clink out of the machines. I'm not sure I'll ever get used to those electronic beeps. But not even the modern recycling system was taking care of the cigarette smoke. In a blue-collar town like Seavy Village, card players get nervous when more than $50 is on the line.

That night, forty players had signed up for the tournament, and the pot tipped a grand for the first time since the casino opened.

***

I'LL LEAVE OUT THE DETAILED DESCRIPTIONS of the rounds, although I can recite all of it, every card, every bet, from the first round, the semi-final round, and the buy-back round. I know by what percentage Tigo beat the odds when he doubled down on eighteen and got a three. I know the exact moment luck abandoned Cherise, and it wasn't when she drew a twenty to the dealer's twenty-one. I even know that I made a small mistake on the twenty-ninth hand, and if the cards hadn't gone my way, I would have been out—deservedly so—and it would have peeved me to no end.

I rarely make mistakes.

I can't afford it.

No. I won't say much about the game except that tempers flared early, even among the regulars, because of the amount of money on the table. And people left angry when they were eliminated because everyone could taste their share of the pot.

When it came to the final hand, only the players and the regulars were left.

Tigo and I were on the table, of course, along with the idiot Joey whose luck was running better than usual, and Smoky Butler who was a dealer at another casino on the other side of the coast range. The rest of the players weren't regulars. Two were bad betters and even worse strategists who managed to get the right cards at the right time, and the other one was a black-haired woman who'd caught all of our attention.

She looked like she should be in Monte Carlo, not Seavy Village, Oregon. She wore a black cocktail dress cut in a modified v that revealed more cleavage than I had seen in years. Her hair was pulled into a chignon and over it she wore a cloche hat complete with small veil. Her lips were dark red, and she smoked a cigarette through a cigarette holder.

And she wasn't lucky.

She was good.

Almost as good as me.

The cards were running hot and cold that night, and our pal Joey's luck ran out first. He was off the table in five hands. Then we lost the first of the two bad betters.

The second was holding in, but not worth our time. He was out by the eleventh hand.

The rest of us, though. The rest of us had a game.

For our buy-in, the casino gives us $500 in tournament chips (which you can't carry to the real tables) per game. The winner, of course, is the person with the most chips after fifteen hands.

By end of the eleventh hand, I had fifteen hundred eighty-five dollars in phony chips.

Tigo had fifteen hundred seventy-five.

Smoky Butler had fifteen hundred and fifty.

And the woman, well, she had two thousand even.

For the first time since I'd left Nevada, I was in a blackjack game where everyone knew how to play. That meant they knew how to draw cards, they knew how to bet, and they knew strategy.

I damned near licked my lips and rubbed my hands together in glee. Instead, I crouched over my chips as if I were protecting them from prying eyes.

We all put out our bets.

The lady put out a hundred.

Smoky put out a hundred and fifty.

Tigo a hundred and twenty-five.

And me, a hundred and fifteen.

Then Rosco, the dealer, began the hand. I was first base (a revolving position), and he gave me an ace of clubs.

Followed by an ace of diamonds for Tigo, an ace of spades for Smoky, and an ace of hearts for the lady.

"They should be playing poker," someone said from behind me.

Rosco gave himself a three of hearts. Then he reached toward the shoe for my next card.

At that moment, the lights went out. The place was pitch black except for several small red dots made by the tips of a hundred cigarettes. I fell across my cards and chips, and Rosco yelled, "Freeze!" to the tournament players. The pit bosses were yelling and the dealers were shouting orders, and some old lady near the slots was wailing at the top of her lungs.

All the time, I kept thinking that this shouldn't be happening. It couldn't be happening. The casino had generators. They should have kicked in. (At the time, I didn't know they'd already kicked in, which meant that they shouldn't have gone off—at least, not all at once.)

Then the lights came back up, or I thought they did, until I realized that the overhead lights in the casino were white, not green. Everyone looked as if they were peering at each other through a fish tank. Even the mystery lady looked green. She was holding her cigarette holder over her chips, and glaring at us all angrily, as if we had caused the problem.

The pit bosses were looking mighty scared. I don't know how much money they had to protect, in chips mostly because the cash disappeared into slots beneath the tables, but I knew it was a lot. And there were more civilians in the casino than pit bosses. Security guards had stationed themselves near the casino banks, and other employees had fanned themselves around the room.

I had never seen anything like it, but it made sense. The casino had to have a drill policy for all types of emergencies.

The place was hot and smoky and everything was green. I kept my hands over my chips and scanned for the source of the light.

As I did, a wind came up. First it licked my hair—or what's left of it—and then it cleared the smoke. At first, I thought the air recycling system had turned back on. Then I realized something greater was happening here.

The source of the green lights were small dervishes the size of my coffee saucers at home. They looked like the alien spaceship out of *E.T.*, only shrunk down into toy specials for MacDonalds' Happy Meals. Except they worked. Their top was a dark cone, and their base was a rotating series of lights, all various shades of green.

And there must have been thousands of them in that small space. Maybe even millions of them.

They hovered over various tables, avoided the slot machines, and disappeared into the back. The poker room was filled with them. I could see them from my vantage points, lined up like tiny aircraft carriers facing a city, the poker players backing against the wall, hands up.

Five crafts found their places over our table, and a sixth placed itself above the dealer. The woman pulled a small pistol from her handbag, and a pit boss immediately grabbed it from her—firearms are illegal on Indian land. He pointed it, wobbling for a moment, at one of the little crafts, then Rosco said,

"If you shoot one and it explodes and we get that green goo all over us and we die, you're going to regret that."

"He'll regret it more if the bullet hits one of us," Smoky said.

"It could ricochet," Tigo added.

The pit boss let the weapon fall to his side. The woman glared at him.

"I wouldn't have missed," she said, as if she blamed him for taking away her opportunity.

The little crafts were above us, whirling and creating the breeze. Rosco had his hand on the money slot. So, it seemed, did every other dealer in the place. We all stared at the things.

"What are they?" Tigo whispered.

I took the question as rhetorical, and apparently everyone else did too because no one answered him.

One of the pit bosses was on the phone, talking with the 911 dispatch. He was whispering loudly, so loudly he may as well have been shouting: "No, really, I'm not kidding. Please…"

Aside from the whirs, the soft mumbles of scared patrons, and the wailing woman, the casino was eerily quiet. No electronic beeps and buzzes, no blaring music, no tinkling chords of winning slots. The silence unnerved me more than anything.

"What do they want?" Tigo whispered.

"Ask them," Smoky snapped.

"I feel like I'm in a James Bond movie," the woman said, and that started a ripple of panic through the pit bosses. They apparently hadn't thought of the things as high tech theft devices.

"If you were in a James Bond movie, my dear," I said, "you'd have better lighting." No one looked good in that ugly green. Not even the most beautiful woman in the place.

Then, as if on cue, green lights flared out of the bottom of the tiny crafts. I backed away from the table, chips forgotten. So did everyone else. Rosco let go of his hold on the money slot, and one of the pit bosses screamed at him but—I noted—did not make a move toward the money, the table or any of the lights.

The lights hit the table and I expected to see big burning holes appear. I was ready to run for cover—all of this going through my mind in the half second it took, mind you—when I realized what was going on.

The cards rose off the surface, whirling and twirling as if they were in a tornado. For a moment, the entire casino was filled with swirling cards. It looked like an elaborate fan dance, or as if green sea gulls were swarming the beach or like an electronic kaleidoscope performance designed especially for us.

Then one by one the cards slid into the crafts through a slot in the sides. They made a slight ca-thunk! as they entered. Then the green tractor lights—what else could they be called?—went out, and the little green ships whirled away.

The doormen and the folks in the parking lot at the time all say the little ships sped out the doors and into a larger ship that had been hovering over the ocean. A number of green slots opened on it, letting the little ships through, and then they disappeared into the night.

The ocean, which had been dark, regained its luminescence, and slowly the lights flickered on all over town.

At least, that's what the outdoor folks said.

Inside, it was chaos. People started shouting and screaming, and that wailing woman continued. A few people stampeded toward the door, and one relatively fit young man got trampled just enough to later attempt a suit against the casino.

Then the lights came back on. The slot machines groaned as they started up, then beeped through their start-up protocol. The slot players, the video poker players, and the keno players all continued with their games except for a few sensible folks who decided to call it a night and left.

I have no idea what happened inside the poker room, but at the tournament table, we counted our chips. The pit bosses put the game on hold as they made sure the money was fine.

It soon became clear the only thing missing from the casino were the cards.

All of them.

Including the decks stored in the back rooms, and the discards waiting to be trucked off the place, and even the little souvenir cards in the gift shop.

Gone.

All gone.

The pit boss who had called 911 was off the phone, saying the police were going to arrive soon, but I suspected it would take them some time. If, as people were saying, things were a mess all over town, it would take the police a while to get anywhere.

"We still have money on the table," Smoky said.

"And a game to finish," Tigo said.

"How do you propose we do that with no cards?" Rosco asked.

"We know what was dealt," the woman said

"But we don't know the order in the rest of the shoe," I said.

"We're going to shuffle a new shoe and start over," Rosco said, "just as soon as we get cards."

"We need the other three players," Tigo said. I glanced around me. Joe was standing behind me as he usually did after he got knocked out of a tournament, but the others were nowhere to be seen.

"We're going to have to put this game on hold until the cops arrive anyway," the pit boss said.

"Until we get cards," Rosco added.

"Besides, everyone'll have to report what they saw," Smoky said.

At that point, the woman and I both stood up. "I think my luck has just run out," the woman said.

"Mine, too," I said.

We left the table and headed toward the door.

"Hey!" Tigo said behind us. "We can't replay the game without you guys!"

"I think the game is forfeit," the woman said.

"Yeah, have the casino put the pot in for next week," I said, knowing they never would.

Then she and I walked through the casino, side by side. The conversations were strangely muted, only a few people discussing what they saw. As we stepped outside, we ran into chaos, cars cramming the parking lot, attendants staring at the sky, a warm bath of light all over the town.

A familiar bath of light.

I had missed it more than I realized.

I turned to her. "There's a nice coffee place about a block from here. Care for a walk?"

"I'd love it," she said.

And we had a nice cup of coffee, and a nice evening, and a nice night, and an even better morning. I never learned her name and she never learned mine, but we both knew that we had left the casino for the exact same reason.

We didn't need to see the police.

Or the media.

Or anyone else, for that matter.

"What do you think they wanted with the cards?" she asked long around midnight.

"I don't know," I said. "Maybe they use bigger shoes than we do."

And a little later, I said, "That, by far, has to be the strangest thing I ever saw in a casino."

"Really?" she responded. "I've seen stranger."

But she never elaborated and I didn't ask her to.

Some stories are better kept close to the vest.

You see, that isn't the strangest thing I'd ever seen in a casino either.

But it's the only one I'll admit to.

And I only do that because I'm a regular and it's a shared group experience. A bit of local legend—the one game that never finished, the pot that got away.

Well away. The casino had to shut down both the poker and blackjack tables for two days while it ordered cards from all over the country. During that time, regulars gave interviews on every show from *CNN* to *Inside Edition*. Except for me.

I laid low for a while even after my lady left. Laid low and watched the skies.

And wondered—

What would have happened on the thirteenth hand if we had all blackjacked on the twelfth?

What would have happened then?

Going Native

GOD, COULD YOU FIND A DULLER WAY TO TRAVEL?" asks my leggy companion, the luscious Ruth. She has this weekend off, and she insisted on coming with me on my assignment. It'll be fun, she said, and then followed that up with, how can I know what you're doing unless I come along with you on occasion? I listened to the logic of that, and now I find myself trapped in a 5' by 6' moving room with a woman who finds train travel passé.

Me, I'm afraid that the Amtrak trip up the mountain will be the best part of this assignment. I work for eight online editors, and all of them called me last week to ask for an article on the annual TVS convention. Such a uniformity of requests has only happened once before in my career, and that was when a woman that I sat beside in grade school, tormented in middle school, and dated in high school was inaugurated as president of the United States. Suddenly my memoirs had value.

Somehow, I doubt that this essay has the same sort of import.

I also had my doubts about bringing Ruth to kooks-ville and now, when we're still two hours away from our destination, I know I've made the Wrong Decision. She is lying on the bottom berth, her bare feet against the dirty plastic wall, her skirt pooled around her waist, and she is not thinking of sex.

Neither am I.

"I mean, we've been on this train for *hours*. How did people travel like this?"

They made love, they ate, they read books. But I do not tell Ruth that. She would see it as a slap, an insult to her great intelligence. In real life, Ruth is a receptionist for a lawyer, but she prefers to call herself a paralegal. She uses legalese, mispronouncing most of it, and pretends that she knows as much as someone who has a law degree.

I've never told her about mine. But then, why should I? It would ruin the sleazy nature of the relationship, the fact that I'm dating her for her deliciously man-made breasts and she's dating me because I know the secrets of the universe.

She believes that's because I'm a journalist. The old-fashioned print kind, even though what we print is done online. I'm paid by the download, which is why I'm on this train trip instead of say, investigating the latest bombing in downtown Seattle. No matter how idealistic you start, you soon learn that it's paranoia that sells.

Which is why we're on a train instead of teleport-ing. There are no teleportation stations in this part of the Cascades. Rumor has it that the first teleportation technician who ventured into this part of Oregon was shot. Whether he lived or died depends on which rumor you believe.

Ruth knew we were heading into no man's land when she decided to come with me, but the closer we get the less I believe she actually *understood* it. I think she thought we'd look at the crazy yokels and then go home.

I think I thought she could handle anything.

Check that. I think I knew, deep down, she was contemplating Marriage, and I wanted to convince her that breaking up was her idea. But that's hindsight. Going in, I was simply concerned about the lack of sex.

"Once," I say, gazing out the window at the snow beside the tracks, "this was the fastest way to travel in the whole world."

"Yeah." She flops an arm over her eyes, missing the deer that stand by a group of trees, staring at us. A 19th century vision in the 21st. "Sad, isn't it?"

I'm not sure. I'm enough of a romantic to enjoy the view. I'm enough of a romantic to wish that she'd enjoy it with me.

***

THE ASSIGNMENT, IF YOU LOOK AT IT historically (which is one of the few things that I've retained from law school, a sense of historical perspective), is a perennial: Go look at the fringe and report back to the masses. Around the turn of the last century, that meant going to carnivals and fairs to examine the bearded women, the two-headed chickens, and the stillborn fetuses that looked like fish. In my grandfather's day, a reporter on this beat might go to see the mysterious Area 51, thought to be a repository for Unidentified Flying Objects (things so familiar they were known by their acronym UFO) and for the little green men who flew them. Me, I get assigned the annual meeting of the Teleportation Victims Society whose own acronym is TVS, but who is known in newsrooms nationwide as TVSo?. I should've known I was in trouble when I tried to explain this little joke to Ruth and she'd stared at me blankly, not even threatening to smile.

The TVSo?s meet every year in Harbor, Oregon, which used to be a 1990s survivalist camp between Bend and Klamath Falls. The area's only attraction, or so I could glean before I arrived, is that it has no teleportation station, and none is planned. If someone wants to travel in that part of the Cascade Range, they either have to go to Bend, fifty miles to the north, or Klamath Falls, over 60 miles to the south. Then they have to take whatever ground transportation is available, provided, of course, they can get it. Amtrak still serves this part of the country, partly because the sparse population can't justify the teleportation system, and partly because the tracks have existed for nearly two hundred years. It's the only form of public transportation between those two stations, and mostly it's used by the low-income folks who can't afford the cost of speedier travel.

I insisted on taking the train all the way from Seattle, over Ruth's protests, because I wanted my experience at the annual meeting to reflect the experience of all the other TVSo?s. I had secretly hoped I'd meet a few of them on this ride, but Ruth has kept me chained to the room, demanding room service, and not paying for it in the way that I had hoped.

Still I manage to sneak to the club car once, and there I see exactly what I expect, a group of tired, smelly people, most of whom are too drunk to look at the magnificent scenery whizzing past. I realize that, in my new khakis and bomber jacket, I am overdressed and as conspicuous as a rich man in Olympia. No one will talk to me. They barely manage to look at me.

And, for the first time, I worry about how I'll pull this assignment off.

***

I SHOULD SAY AT THIS STAGE of article research, I always worry about how I'll pull the assignment off. Even though what I write is dictated into my wrist-top, edited on a larger screen at home, and e-mailed directly to my editor, what I do is really not much different from the work, say, Mark Twain did almost two hundred years ago. He ventured out into places unknown and reported back.

Ernest Hemingway did that, so did Ernie Pyle, and Peter Arnett. The great journalists thrived in times of war. When there is no war—or no war America is interested in—we are stuck with perennials. And no journalist ever became famous by risking his life at a TVSo? convention.

I simply want to go in, find a few things that are amusing, see if I can discover the secret behind the victimology, and return to home base with all parts intact. I know that, by Sunday evening, I will have a story. I'm just not sure if it's the kind of story Hemingway would have dispatched from Spain.

In fact, I know it's not the moment the train pulls into Harbor, Oregon.

***

WHEN RUTHIE AND I GET OFF THE TRAIN at the small white station nestled against a snow-covered ridge, we are greeted like visiting royalty. I made no secret of my job as a journalist, but it's really Ruthie they want to see. It seems, on the e-slip she sent with her fee, that she listed her employment as she always does.

A paralegal and a journalist. We are a dream couple for the TVSo?s.

I am not the only journalist in this place. Every major television reporter, radio commentator, vid producer, and holotechnician is here to record the loonies in action. I am one of the few print people, and the only one with enough awards to make me semi-famous. Every TVSo? wants to tell me his story, to introduce me to little Jonnie or Suzy or Uncle Billy, and to show me what makes them different.

When I get off the train, I realize I am not ready for this. The grasping hands, the slightly desperate gaze. I insist on going to the hotel before meeting people, and Ruth gives me her I-can't-believe-you're-doing-this look. That's when I realize she's not upset about the location or the people. She's upset that I want to leave them. She not only relishes the attention, she believes she can give these people advice. She doesn't realize how dangerous the situation can be. She's with the only people in the world who might take her seriously. I grip her arm and follow our host to the Compound, our hotel.

The Compound was the former survivalist's camp, and looks it. The outbuildings are made of wood hammered together by people who clearly didn't know what they were doing. The main building, where the restaurant and gift shop reside, was once a ranch-style house, built in the mid-twentieth century, complete with front-facing garage. The building had been added onto, once during its survivalist camp days—that was evident by the concrete bunker in the back—and once by the hotel, the brass and wood façade that tried to make everything upscale.

Our room isn't really a room. It was cabin Number 8. A plaque on the door tells us that it had once been used by the house's original owners as a storage shed, and was remodeled into a cabin when the camp started in the early 1980s. The plaque tells us proudly that eight people lived in this space; I'm wondering how Ruth and I will manage for a weekend.

The room is square, with an area carved out for a bathroom with an ancient shower and plastic tub. The sink has motion detectors instead of computer controls, and the toilet actually has a handle for flushing. Ruth is charmed, but I wonder if that will last into the middle of the night, when one of us stumbles in there and initiates the gurgle and grunt of the ancient plumbing.

We unpack, and then Ruth wants to reenter the fray. I'm more interested in checking out the dining facilities. The reconstituted chicken I had on the train didn't last me long.

Outside, we see several blue-and-white signs, pointing to various cabins. Most signs are hand-lettered and made specifically for the conference: Registration is to our left; Legal advice is to our right; and Testimonials is straight ahead. Other signs show us the way to improve our Education, covering everything from Technological Secrets to the History of Transportation. Many of these, I know, are ongoing programs, and I will check them out through the weekend. It's the guest speakers I am most interested in, and those are going to be the hardest events to see.

***

IN THE REGISTRATION LINE I learn that the TVSo?s aren't all low-income poorly educated folks like the research had led me to expect. The man in front of me is a doctor from Philadelphia who has documentation on "differences" and was willing to call it up on his wrist-top right there in the frigid Oregon mud. The slender, pretty woman behind me is a reasonably well known vid personality whose career went into a decline, she says, after she teleported 65 times in one month. I talk to both of them at some length. Ruth has left me alone in line while she went on to the lodge for drinks.

She has been gone a long time.

I draw the same sort of crowd I drew at the train station. I am uncomfortable, used to being the observer, not the observed. Everyone wants to tell me a story; everyone wants me to know how teleportation changes people, how it creates differences where there were none before.

Some of the stories are just silly, like the vid personality's. She claims she lost a little bit of charisma each time she teleported from one place to another. Some are strange, like the woman who has me examine holograms of her now-estranged husband, a man whose eye color changed in the space of one afternoon from green to brown.

The rest are merely sad. Many are from people who claim that their spouses are no longer the same people they married, and they blame use of public teleportation. Others show evidence of medical conditions they claim were caused by teleporting, and still some have tales of close loved ones who died soon after traveling in a teleportation device.

I have read the literature; I am familiar with all variations on these stories and more. I even know their origins.

I ask the eye color woman why she believes her husband's eyes were the only thing to change.

"I didn't say they were the only thing, now did I?" she says angrily.

I turn away, afraid to follow up.

***

THE FIRST BIG BREAKTHROUGH in teleportation occurred in the late 1990s when a team of Austrian scientists successfully completed a transfer on the sub-atomic level. The physics of the breakthrough was too complex to explain to the layman in the popular newspapers of the day, so many journalists attempted [unsuccessfully] to put the discovery in layman's terms.

I have tried to hunt down the origin of the example used for the laymen and have been, to date, unsuccessful. I suspect either one of the scientists got exasperated with the journalists' stupid questions and used the example to explain, poorly, what was going on, or a journalist attempted to translate what he thought he understood into language that he thought other people could understand.

Their experiment, said the news organizations of the day, was as if the scientists had taken a red ball in one room, made it disappear, and then reappear in another room—although what was teleported was not the ball itself, but the *quality* of redness which was then transferred onto another ball.

It is not what we experience. We experience the teleportation first imagined in pulp fiction stories of over a hundred years ago. Our bodies literally disassemble in one location, are transferred to another location, and are then reassembled. There are documented cases of malfunctions, most dating from the early days of the technology and almost all of them having to do with apes who arrived dead. These deaths were not pretty or simple: they had to do with parts being reassembled in the wrong order, rather like taking a puzzle apart, then trying to put it together by placing all the corners in the middle. Those details were resolved long before any human being stepped onto a teleportation pad. The things we must worry about are simpler: power failures and computer malfunctions, both of which can lose us mid-transfer. This problem is the greatest in Third World countries, in devices built out of scrap metal, most likely, by the operator's Uncle Ralph. Teleportation is not sanctioned to those countries, or is done purely at the user's own risk. Here and in "approved" countries, every device is scrutinized, overhauled, and replaced more often than anything else in our technologically advanced society.

This is what the literature tells me. It is what exists in all published reports, the meetings before Congress, and in several teleportation companies' legal databases. I know there can be problems—we all do. The problems are called "acceptable risk," something we all assume when we step on a teleportation pad, or even when we walk out our front door. What varies from person to person is how acceptable some risks are.

It is the idea that we can be disassembled and reassembled that unnerves people the most. A large number of people (actual estimates vary, depending on the reporting agency) refuse to use teleportation, allowing other forms of mass transit to remain in business. Most of these people are not TVSo?s. They simply don't like the idea of being taken apart and put back together without it being necessary, and are not willing to sacrifice their original unity for the sake of instantaneous travel.

Others cannot imagine traveling any other way. Frequent teleporters receive a discount on each trip. "Frequent" is defined in the industry as anyone making more than ten trips per day. I have only hit the ten trip in one day milestone once, and it left me feeling disoriented and unnerved—not, I hasten to add, because I was disassembled so many times, but because, after five different teleportation stations, I lost track of my surroundings. Later I learned that frequent travelers set their wrist-top to remind them of their location and their purpose for being there upon arrival.

I have read all the literature, examined all the records, and while I still feel a twinge of nerves when I step on the platform, I prefer the instantaneous shift, the delight at having been in Manhattan one moment and Rome the next. It is not different, my grandmother once told me, than that frisson of fear she used to feel whenever an airplane's wheels left the ground or whenever a train went over a particularly high and narrow bridge.

It is human nature to worry about the accidental, the unexpected, the unknown. It is also human nature to magnify those things into problems so strange as to be somehow plausible.

***

THE TVSo?s HAVE THREE BANQUETS at their week-end meeting, and I have bought tickets to all three. Ruth did not want to eat at the banquets. In fact, she soon made it clear that she did not want to spend time with me. She says my attitude is too cynical, my remarks too cutting. She is already right. I am already thinking in the tone I've decided to take for this article, a tone that my brain established while part of it tried to concentrate on the seriousness of the vid personality's loss of charisma.

The first banquet is on Friday night, and there I am happily surprised. The food is excellent. It is free-range chicken, brought in from a nearby ranch, local vegetables grown and stored here, marinated in local wine, mixed with spices grown in the chef's own herb garden.

Nothing was shipped in: no risk of teleportation tainting the food. And somehow it does seem fresher. Or perhaps the chef, a world-renowned man who refused to allow me to use his name in this article, has simply lived up to his spectacular reputation.

The speaker that night is a transportation historian who is, believe it or not, duller than he sounds. He reads his speech off the TelePrompTer modification in his contact lenses, probably much as he does in class, which forces him to stare straight ahead. That, combined with his monotone, makes him seem as if he's teleported one too many times.

The diners at my table, which is toward the back, immediately deduce the problem and begin whispering, as I imagine his students often do. We introduce ourselves and tell each other why we're here.

The woman to my immediate left looks like a Hollywood grandmother, which is to say that she's round, gray-haired and jolly. She confides that she went to see her grandchildren on her only teleportation trip, and instead of arriving in Pittsburgh as planned, she arrived in Philadelphia. The teleportation operators claim she simply told them she was going to Philly, but she claims that they punched in the wrong destination. I take mental notes, knowing that what is at stake here is more than a simple trip. She lives on a fixed income and she scrimped to afford the teleport. She could not afford to then go from Philly to Pittsburgh and back home. She missed a trip, and probably several meals, for that one abortive visit.

This is a problem I can get behind. It is not magic woo-woo incantations in which she claims that she suddenly ballooned in size because her protons expanded or that she got skin cancer that should have belonged to someone else. This is the kind of operator error we all worry about. I have had nightmares about getting on a teleporter in Portland and ending up in Beijing.

The woman next to her confides that there is a lawyer in the legal section who is trying to get enough contacts to initiate a class action suit for just that sort of problem. The grandmother thanks her, and then asks her, whispering politely of course, why she's here. The woman, who is in her mid-forties, has the prettiest lavender hair I've ever seen. She flushes a nice shade of pink that somehow complements the lavender and admits that she would rather not say.

I am beginning to think I've hit a lucky table. Imagine someone who has come to a TVSo? convention who is unwilling to admit why she has come. It is almost antithetical to the purpose of the conference.

I make a mental note to pull her aside later, then ask the man to my right why he has come. "Reporter," he says tersely, not whispering. "Just like you."

He gets shushed by the people at the table behind him, who, believe it or not, are engrossed in the teacher's speech. At that point, I surface briefly, realize the man has droned on for thirty minutes and hasn't yet reached the invention of the automobile. I signal a waiter for more coffee.

The woman to the reporter's right bursts into tears when asked why she's here, and we get shushed again. I actually don't mind because I get an odd sense that the tears are fake. Still, we dutifully lean forward after she dries her eyes with her linen napkin.

"My baby," she whispers, and stifles a sob. The entire table behind us glares at us with angry eyes. We glare back, then lean as close as we can.

"My baby," she says again, "was a boy when he went into the device."

Suddenly I don't want to hear any more, and neither, it seems, does anyone else. The reporter hands her another napkin, and makes sympathetic noises, but as quickly as he politely can, he rises and makes his way to the men's room.

Ten minutes later, when he has not returned and the speaker is rhapsodizing about the uses of airplanes in World War I, I excuse myself. The corridor outside is empty, but I find a new convention going on at the bar.

"I don't know why they invite him back," says one woman to a gale of laughter. It seems that this is the fifth year the historian has spoken on Friday night, and this year he is actually *more* interesting than he has ever been.

One of the conference organizers overhears, and says rather stiffly, "We invite him so that you all have an historical overview of the problems we face."

"Oh," the laughing woman says, "but don't you think that teleportation is a little different than, say, a Model T?"

"No," the organizer says, and I realize that this is one of those dangerous people to whom the phrase "sense of humor" has no meaning at all, "it is all a manifestation of our need to make the world smaller. Once everyone thought that instantaneous travel would solve all our ills. They didn't realize that it would cause more problems than it started."

"Do you believe," one woman asks, "that everyone who has been in a teleportation device is still human?"

Not even the conference organizer answers that question. It is too touchy. Most of the people here are here because they have been in a teleportation device. If the woman's right, that would mean none of us are human. I don't believe that. I believe we're very human, although the more I see, the more I wonder what side of humanity we actually belong to.

***

THE NEXT MORNING, I wander over to Legal, and listen to lawyers pontificate on ways to collect damages from teleportation companies. I hear the familiar litany of successful lawsuits—there aren't many, and most are nuisance cases much like the grandmother's of the night before—but the audience is attentive and asks polite questions.

In the afternoon, I poke my head into Education, and see the historian. I don't run from there, although I'm tempted. I walk slowly, pretending I had ventured into that area by mistake.

Ruth is nowhere to be seen. She did show up in our room the night before, but long after I was asleep, and I thought I smelled brandy, but by that point I didn't really care. I wonder idly who she has found to entertain herself with and how she can use him to further her career. The thought, though accurate, is uncharitable, and I then wonder when I stopped thinking with fondness of Ruth's tendency's to exaggerate and began to be annoyed by them. Probably around the point when her manufactured breasts became her most fascinating feature.

That night's speaker is an expert in teleportation technology and I am assured by almost everyone who's been here before that he makes the historian look glib. I am sorry to give up the free-range chicken, but I cannot bear another two hours trapped in those uncomfortable wooden banquet chairs.

I go into the restaurant, where I've had two delicious breakfasts, and cast about for a table. It seems to have a lot of patrons, considering there is a banquet going on in the next room.

Ruth is at a table near the window. Even though it is dark, I can make out the ghostly shape of the nearby mountain, snow-covered and shiny. She waves me over.

She is sitting with the lawyers. They have asked that no other tables be filled around them, and so far the restaurant is able to comply. Ruth, it seems, has been spending her time with the entire legal wing of this conference and learning "a whole heckuva lot."

I sit down, and listen for a while. This seems like an informal version of the panel I had attended in the morning. I order a steak, and do not ask if it was shipped in or slaughtered locally, for which I am razzed, and then one of the attorneys, an overweight vegetarian who consumes way too much wine during the evening, informs me of the many ways that beef could kill me. Since I have heard this lecture before, I add a few insights of my own, all the while chomping heartily on my dinner.

Finally they ask me why I'm here, and I tell them that I'm a paid observer of human nature.

"He's journalist," Ruth says, breaking my cover.

They eye me as if *I'm* the slimy species and I explain that I'm a practitioner of New Journalism almost a century after New Journalism was introduced. It is my way of gaining legitimacy among the illegitimate: pretend to a literary value that I don't really have.

The New Journalism comment seems to have silenced them, so to break the ice—and to make my dinner worthwhile—I ask them what they really think about teleportation technology.

"It makes lawyers rich!" one of them said and the others laugh. But I press them, and finally a dark-suited man next to Ruth says, "I used to laugh at these folks and then questions started coming up, questions I couldn't get an answer to."

One of the female attorneys nods, and still another, the overweight vegetarian, says, "Yeah, like why is there a ban on kids under the age of three taking teleportation?"

"It's not a firm ban," a New York lawyer says. "You can get around it with a doctor's permission."

"Yeah," the vegetarian says. "Why a doctor? And what does he give permission for?"

"I've never seen any instances of babies traveling. They don't allow it, with or without the doctor," the woman says.

"But I met a woman who says her baby—" I start and they all shake their heads sadly, silencing me.

"She's here every year," the vegetarian says. "I checked the story out. She doesn't have a kid. I don't even think she's female."

They chuckle again, and the joviality is back. No matter how I push them, I can't learn what the other questions are. The vegetarian promises to tell me if I come to the bar later. I do, and he's passed out in a pile of corn chips. I vow to try and find him the following day.

***

THE NEXT MORNING, as the speakers are setting up, I go to the Technological Secrets area. It's in a wide auditorium with holographic capabilities. My mind boggles just at the thought of seeing strange machinery in life-size and 3D.

It takes me a moment to find a speaker who'll talk to me, who doesn't try to get me to wait until his presentation. I tell him about the lawyers' collective unease about the baby ban.

"You ask the teleportation stations they'll tell you it's because babies are too fragile for most kinds of travel. Like they'll ban an infant from a jet." The guy I'm talking to is six feet tall and has a honking nasal voice. I'm glad I elected not to stay for his presentation, even though he seems nice enough. "But it's really because of the stress to the body."

"I thought there is no stress."

He looks at me as if I'm the dumbest thing he's seen at this conference, and given what I've seen, I'm almost

insulted. He holds up a glass of water. "You can't teleport crystal either," he says. "Sometimes it shatters. And
it shouldn't. I mean, they perfected this at the subatomic
level, or so they say."

"You don't think they did?"

"Between you, me, and the wall," he says, "I know
they perfected it. The problem is that they don't use
the right equipment to teleport people. It's like building a house. We can build a damn fine house with everything correct. But we hire contractors who want to
make as much money as possible, and they do it—have
done it—since time immemorial by using inferior parts
and charging the same as they would for good parts. I
try to tell the lawyers that, but it's not glamorous, and
it's damned hard to prove. They tell me they'll help me
when I can show damage caused by inferior parts. I can
show damage. I just can't make a credible link."

Later that day, I check his statements with a few other technology wonks. They agree that the problem with
public teleportation is that it's *public*. The system used
by the President and other heads of state is state-of-the-
art, so protected that nothing can go wrong. The system
used by the rest of us, well, these guys would have us
all believe it's held together by spit and glue and pieces
manufactured just after the turn of the century.

It makes me think of all those bans on teleportation
travel to third-world countries. If our technology is bad,
what is the technology like that was hammered together
by someone's Uncle Ralph? The very idea raises images of

those poor puzzle box monkeys with the corners where their middle should be.

Of course when I get back home, and call the various teleportation manufacturers, they all give me the company line and swear teleportation is the safest form of transportation since walking. Even that can go wrong, I say. Think of potholes. Think of missteps, twisted ankles and tripping over small children. But the manufacturers don't find me funny. When I get belligerent, forgetting, for a moment that this is supposed to be a puff piece and not investigative reporting, they transfer me to their legal departments who remind me of libel laws and how careful I need to be in questioning their companies.

***

THE FREE-RANGE CHICKEN IS GONE by the third banquet, but the speaker is delightful. He's a comedian just starting out, and he proves to me that the TVSo?s have a sense of humor, since most of his jokes are aimed at them, and they laugh uproariously. I don't. I feel vaguely embarrassed, mostly because I know I would have laughed if I'd been watching this guy in any other setting but this one.

As I head out, I look for Ruth. She's still surrounded by her lawyers, and when she sees me, she waves me over. She puts a hand on the overweight vegetarian's arm and informs me that he has hired her as a paralegal. I pull her aside, remind her that jobs aren't always that easy to come by and that she'd better check his credentials. She frowns at me, asks me if I think she's dumb or something—a question which I decline to answer—and then stalks off. I gather, from that whole exchange, that she's not taking the train home, and I turn out to be right. My wish has been granted. She has forgotten thoughts of Marriage and believes that our break-up is her idea. I find that I regret the whole plan, not because I wanted to marry her, but because I had hoped that I would at least get to try all parts of train travel, from meal to sleep to sex. We had neglected sex on the way there, and I was hoping for a bit on the way home.

Instead, I spend the next week finding a way to ship her clothes cheaply without using teleportation technology, since the vegetarian likes to keep his office "pure."

I am beginning to understand the sentiment. My moment of hesitation as I step on the teleportation platform in Bend—I see no point in train travel all the way to Seattle if I'm not going to be able to have nookie in transit—lasts nearly three minutes, and customers behind me get angry. But I keep thinking of those banned babies, and Uncle Ralph, and inferior-grade equipment, and the way that the sheet rock in my condo flakes like someone's untended dandruff, and I find myself more and more reluctant to travel in that instantaneous sort of way. After all, why am I in such a hurry? I'm a journalist, for godssake, a man who makes his living off observing, and observation is something that can't be rushed. I am proud of my observation skills, and proud of my capability for contemplation that makes them possible.

But what I've been observing since I got back is my own reflection in the mirror. There's a line down one side of my face, an instant wrinkle that really doesn't look like a laugh line or something that would naturally occur as I age. It looks more like a fold, or a crease, something incorrectly ironed in, as if a section of me were miscut and hemmed wrong.

I never noticed the wrinkle before getting on that teleportation station in Bend. I have been obsessed with it since. And I think, I really think, that my obsession is a product of the TVSo? convention, but not for the reason that you'd think. It's not that I suddenly believe the teleporter has given me a new wrinkle. It's just that I find the idea of a wrinkle induced from the outside better than the idea that I'm growing older. It's easier to believe in the fiction. It's nicer.

It takes the responsibility for that particular line off me.

Or at least, that's what I tell myself. Because I do need to teleport on occasion for my job. Journalists observe, yes. But they must observe in the right places. And when my editor tells me to get to London yesterday, I do the next best thing. I get there two minutes from now, new wrinkles be damned.

But I find that I do examine mirrors more, and I wonder, when I think something particularly cruel, like most of my thoughts about Ruth lately, if I've become less than human. Is humanity something we can lose, little bit by little bit, like the vid personality and her charisma? And if so, how can we tell it's gone? Is it replaced by paranoia, by worry, in equal degrees? And am I, in worrying about this, showing signs of latent TVSo?ism?

I don't know. But I do suspect that my recent desire to take the train to the far reaches of the United States has less to do with my unfulfilled sexual fantasy than it does with my desire to avoid a technology that I may have learned to fear. Then I remind myself of the history of this form of paranoia; I know that being a reporter from the fringe requires an ability to cross over into that land and appear to be a native. I'm simply afraid I've taken it too far. Going native requires residency in kooksville, and while it only takes an instant to reach that particular destination, it takes years and expensive psychotherapy to get out.

***

When I turned in this essay, I thought of asking for a bonus, a sort of combat pay to compensate for the wrinkle, for the increased harassment as I take an extra minute of other people's time while I hesitate before stepping on a teleportation platform.

But my editor vid-conferenced with me this morning, wanting to discuss what he calls "proper compensation." My article, he says—(this thing you are currently reading, without this coda)—has given him an idea. Teleportation has overtaken other forms of transportation so much that his younger readers have probably never flown in a plane or driven a car. He wants me to do these things, and report back about my experiences, as if I have gone to yet another frontier, even if it is a part of the past.

He asks what I want to do first, and then reminds me this will be on the magazine's expense.

"A ticket on the Orient Express," I say.

"Ah," he says. "You'll title it 'Strangers on a Train?'"

I'm thinking not of Patricia Highsmith and Alfred Hitchcock, but of luscious, willing blonds with breasts the size of helium balloons and the ca-thunk, ca-thunk of the wheels on a track suggesting a rhythm that no teleportation device can hope to match.

"I hope so," I say, and realize this is the kind of fringe I like. "I certainly hope so."

The Amazing Quizmo

*D*ARREN WORKS AS QUIZMASTER at local bars. He has an empire: five bars rotate his services and one, the Triangle, promotes his appearances heavily. When he works, he is no longer Darren. He is Quizmo The Great God of Answers, and woe to all who doubt his superiority.

In real life, Darren works as a bike messenger, pedaling across Portland to deliver important packages. Usually he leaves his helmet on when he takes a package inside a building, worried that one of his regular quiz participants will see him and realize that the Great God of Answers doesn't know how to get a Real Job.

The rest of the time, he trolls Internet cafes for esoteric information. He can't afford an Internet hookup in his two-room apartment (a deluxe studio, the landlord calls it), so he must do his online work elsewhere.

He doesn't approach anyone. Even when he's running the quizzes, he doesn't socialize. Between rounds, he plays music—mostly to annoy—and he rarely leaves the mike stand. When he's on his bike, he says hello to no one. He delivers his packages and leaves.

This morning's package goes to a law firm in one of the hoity toity doorman buildings that recently opened in the Pearl. The Pearl used to be the worst section of downtown. Now it's exclusive, and pretends to be part of a larger city, like New York.

But the Pearl is not New York. Doormen still don't know how to act. They pretend like their job is important—they half-bow to people coming in, offer to help the residents with baggage, smile at anyone dressed in a suit. They also scowl at the messengers, not realizing that in a real city, bike messengers are treated with respect.

As Darren saunters in, holding up the manila envelope and saying loudly, "Package for Hanley, Hanley, Combs and Whitmore," he realizes that the doorman scowling at him is Yukio, one of his best players—a member of the team Brainiacs that plays at Buzzard Bill's on Wednesday nights.

Darren's stomach turns. Yukio is an excellent observer as well as a good player, a competitive man who seems to blame Darren whenever the Brainiacs lose.

Darren keeps his sunglasses on as well as his helmet, glad he wore the chinstrap today because it hides his trademark wispy goatee.

"Can't let you in, buddy," Yukio says in a decidedly unfriendly tone. "I'll make sure they get the package."

And you get the tip, Darren thinks but doesn't say because as a messenger, he tries not to have the same edge he has as Quizmo.

"Sorry," he says even though he isn't. Half the messengers in the city fall for this crap from doormen and building security, and it isn't right. Tips are part of the job. "Got to give it directly to the client."

Yukio grabs his arm. "No can do, kid. Not without I.D. and approval."

Darren shakes free, sighs loudly, and hands over his messenger I.D. No photograph—none needed—and his real name, which no one in the bars know. To them, the mighty Quizmo is a person with only one name, like Madonna, only a little prettier and a lot smarter.

Yukio takes the I.D., looks at it for a moment, then hands it back to Darren, the battle lost.

Darren walks to the elevator, his cleated shoes clicking on the brand-new marble. He gets the floor number from the digital information board which lists all the businesses and coyly states that Floors 6-14 are residential, without revealing any resident names at all.

The gold-edged mirrored doors ping open and as he steps on, he sees himself, and realizes that, in his get-up, he doesn't look like a small Lance Armstrong, but like a subspecies of insect, something with a carapace over its head and probably multiple lenses in its non-human eyes.

No wonder no one smiles and nods at him as he rides by. They see him as something other, something alien, something inexplicably frightening. They don't realize that under the spandex and messenger company logos is a man who, at thirty-five, still doesn't know what to do with his life and is hoping that somewhere, somehow, he will be discovered for the genius that he is.

The elevator stops with a bounce that new equipment shouldn't have. The doors open, and he gets off on a generic floor with 21st century brown carpets and off-white walls, with poster art that someone thoughtfully signed so that it would be more expensive than hotel art, and rows and rows of dark brown fire doors, each with the plaque that announces some corporate name.

He immediately turns right, even though he hasn't been on this floor before, because law offices with names that big often have the largest door with the most space and the best entry.

He's not disappointed. Hanley, Hanley, Combs and Whitmore have a wooden plaque on their brown door announcing their extreme importance, and as he pushes the door open, he steps into a world of glass that overlooks the Pearl and all its pie-in-the-sky condo construction. Maybe the view'll be pretty some day. Right now, it's just the same as views from high rises in Chicago and Dallas and Los Angeles, except that the receptionist doesn't wear makeup and has on Birkenstocks that match her simple blue dress.

She is authorized to take the package and give him his tip. Apparently Hanley, Hanley, Combs and Whitmore have an account with the messenger service, because all she does is sign the company invoice and hand it to him, tip already tallied.

He suppresses his bitter response. He wouldn't've fought with Yukio if he'd known he'd get the standard tip.

It's low—about seven dollars—and certainly not worth the hassle or the lost time for his other packages.

Still, he says thanks like a good drone and clatters his way to the elevator and Yukio.

Yukio doesn't even notice Darren as he steps off the elevator and makes his way outside. No good-bye, no sportsman-like "Next Time!", nothing.

If Darren had known Yukio was this rude, Darren would've never let Yukio have an extra thirty seconds in last week's Impossible Round.

Darren shakes his head as he gets on his bike.

People. They're never what you want them to be.

***

THAT NIGHT, HE APPEARS at the Triangle. The Triangle is Portland's best gay bar, some say the best gay bar on the entire West Coast. It's downtown, near the Pearl but not of the Pearl, and has bleached wood tables, found-art glassware and collages hanging on the walls.

It took Darren weeks to get used to working here—the occasional pinch on the ass from men who look like they could break him in half; the kissing women who don't do it for titillation, like they do on the late night porn programs he pays too much of his messenger money for; the ultra-stylish clothing favored by half the clientele and the worker-bee anti-style clothing favored by the rest.

At first, he thought they'd see him for what he is, an imposter who has no one—gay or straight—waiting for him when he gets home, a man who doesn't know how to pick up anyone of either gender, a man who isn't even sure he has a gender because nothing—and no one—has interested him in years.

But once he made it clear he wasn't there to meet men or influence people, once he took control As A Professional, the clientele of the Triangle accepted him as one of their own—or maybe a little more than one of their own. Here they don't like calling him Quizmo—they think it's too country-western. Here they call him the Quizmaster with a little more relish than he would like.

The Triangle also provides his best teams. People pay more attention here; they're less drunk and better educated than the teams at the other bars. So he always puts on his best material, the stuff that stumped the other players. When he comes to the Triangle late on Thursday nights, he has his A game, practiced and polished and ready to defeat the masses.

Tonight he doesn't feel on his A game even though he has his A material. It's been a good week. His favorite teams won at each bar, and he hasn't helped them along in any way. He found little pieces of information that no one else seems to know on an obscure website from England, and he finally got his DVDs of *Remington Steele*'s third season, which he'd ordered back in July.

So he should be happy, anticipating the clash of minds that always happens at the Triangle. Instead, he's still thinking about Yukio, how that man bruised his arm trying to steal his tip, and wondering how he will react when he sees Yukio again.

The Triangle provides Darren with a little booth right in the middle of the dance floor. The booth dates from the 1980s, when the Triangle was a dying disco bar, and with the touch of a button, Darren can fill the place with flashing lights. Before he arrives, the bar turns on a soft red light over his chair. When he's ready to go, he changes the light to blue. It's annoying and makes the screen of his laptop hard to read, so he also has a tiny desk light that he places just beside the computer, resting the light on the printout of his questions in case the ancient computer bought on the cheap dies.

The format for the quizzes is easy: Players form teams who then compete to answer five rounds of questions. The first round (which he privately calls the Lull Round) is designed to make everyone feel smart. It's the only round in which he uses pop culture questions—and those he usually steals from this week's *People*, which he doesn't even buy, but reads on the grocery store stands every Monday morning when he gets his fruit, yogurt, and Grape Nuts for his daily breakfasts.

The second through fourth rounds are middling hard for anyone with a general college degree. He's found that people who are good in one area (say English Literature) suck at things like Geography and really suck at Science. Still, teams learn to balance such things and long-lasting teams, like the Dominos here or the Brainiacs at Buzzard Bill's, have a good mix of general interest folks and science nerds.

It's the final round, the round he calls the Impossible Round, a phrase stolen from one of the great quizmasters in that quizmaster paradise, Philadelphia, which separates the smart from the brilliant. If teams in the Impossible Round get one question right out of ten, they're doing well. This round benefits only the truly esoteric trivia mind—the kind that, for instance, not only knows the exact date of Stalin's death, but also the day of the week, the hour, the method and the identities of the suspected killers.

Tonight's teams are the long-standing Dominoes and Sherlock Holmes Smarter Sisters (or Shiz for short [Shits, some of the other teams call them as the evening devolves into drunkenness]), as well as the fairly new BeBop Babies and the Woodhull Group. Two other quickly assembled teams died in the second round, unable to respond to any questions once pop culture disappears as a category.

The Dominoes and the Shiz have a year-long rivalry, based mostly on gender. Someone issued the age-old challenge—that boys are smarter than girls or vice versa—and ever since, the rivalry has been intense.

Darren likes it: he likes digging deep into his bag of tricks. He's got the teams figured and he varies the competition. One week, he leans the questions toward the Dominoes, the next toward the Shiz. The win-loss ratio has remained steady, especially in the last six months when he started instituting the alternating week policy.

But tonight, the Shiz have a new team member. Liz is gone, replaced by a woman named Cindy. The name surprises him, which is why he can remember it. She seems too exotic to be a Cindy. She isn't pretty but she's not ugly either. She's *arresting* and as he stares at her throughout the night, he realizes she looks, as Conan O'Brien might say, like the perfect lovechild of K.D. Lang and Lucy Liu. Only an orange scarf, worn babushka-like over her too-short black hair, gives her any mark of normality at all.

She's a ringer. She can answer pop culture questions, science questions, math questions, esoteric religion questions, and history questions, as well as questions about literature, art, and music.

Her knowledge seems as encyclopedic as his and, from a distance, more vast. By the end of round five, she hasn't missed a single question.

This makes him grouchy. He puts on Poison be-tween Round Five and the Impossible Round because he knows the music will piss off everyone in the place. Then he climbs off his chair, steps out of the booth, and heads to the bar.

Everyone watches in surprise. He never goes to the bar.

He can't decide what to order. Should he order liquor straight up? Or should he order a wimpy-ass drink that has umbrellas and lots of sugar to hide the taste?

In the end, he realizes he should order what he wants. In this bar, as opposed to all the other bars in which he works, no one cares what everyone else does.

He gets, of all things, seltzer water because he wants to keep his brain clear, and he gives the bartender a ridiculously large tip. As he turns around, he finds himself surrounded by the Dominoes.

"Cindy shouldn't be allowed to play," says their leader, Genghis. Genghis, of course, isn't his real name, but it's his stage name, just like Quizmo is Darren's.

Darren isn't going to get into this kind of pissing contest. He learned early in his quizmastering days that the composition of the teams—so long as each has no more than six players—is none of his business.

He clutches his seltzer water and tries to push past. Genghis's second, Kubilai steps in front of him. Genghis doesn't scare him—he's smaller than Darren with no muscles to speak of, but Kubilai had been a biker in a previous life and still has the tattoos. He still has the muscles as well, and the shaved head over which Darren had once seen him break a chair.

"Cindy ain't no queer," Kubilai says. "She don't belong here."

"Teams are teams," Darren says, knowing it sounds lame.

He pushes past, remembering now why he never goes to the bar. Usually a cocktail waitress brings him something when he signals. But he felt trapped and a little surprised that Cindy could answer all of his questions. He needed to move to shake off the unease that she had engendered in him.

As he starts up the stairs, she appears beside him. She is big, with huge muscles in her arms, and large breasts that sag the way that real breasts sag. Up close, she looks a little familiar.

"I like your game," she says, leaning on the railing beside the stairs like a groupie.

"Thanks." He keeps his head down. He doesn't want to play favorites.

"I heard it was hard."

He shrugs.

She grins. "Maybe it's just my night."

He feels a flare of anger which he would normally indulge in, but he's still off-balance from the conversation with the Dominoes. Besides, from her perspective, she's right; the game has been easy.

He climbs up the stairs and doesn't look at her. Instead, he punches a few keys on his laptop, calling up the Truly Impossible File, the questions that no one has been able to answer in two years of the game.

He pulls twenty at random, then checks to make sure they cover at least half his categories. He shuts off Poison, changes the lights, and forces everyone back in their seats.

Then he fires off the questions in rapid succession:

—What was the name of Dorothy Parker's first dog?

—What was the chief export of Rome in 1433?

—In what language did the word zenith originate? What was the word's original use and meaning?

Cindy answers all three of the first three questions, but the fourth stops her: What is Fermat's Last Theorem and why is it famous?

Most math people can answer the second part. The theorem is famous because the proof disappeared. But very few people have memorized the theorem itself. Someone on the Shiz thinks she remembers the theorem. The Dominoes argue quietly among themselves.

He hits the timer when no one rings in after four minutes, and for the agonizingly slow sixty seconds that remain, he finds himself twisting his fingers together like an evil wizard.

At least four players in Bailey's Saloon would have been able to answer this question. The only reason it remains in the Truly Impossible File is because the night he asked the question, those players had gotten exceedingly drunk.

In fact, a lot of questions in the Truly Impossible File remain because the teams had too much to drink, something that would never happen here at the Triangle.

The buzzer sounds. Curses echo through the bar and some other patrons applaud, happy to see that not even the Shiz know all the answers this night.

He smiles, feeling superior once more.

Then he leans into his microphone.

"Since none of you losers even tried to answer that question in the time allowed, we'll subtract ten points from both sides."

The groans around the bar please him. He's in his groove again. He asks the next five questions, satisfied that Cindy only gets one right.

Maybe it's just my night indeed. Maybe it was.

But it is no longer.

***

His good mood lasts until three p.m. the next afternoon, a half an hour before his shift ends. He's gets his last package, and realizes that again it goes to Hanley, Hanley, Combs and Whitmore.

He doesn't want to see Yukio, but he has no choice, he's already answered the first half of the call. As he peddles across downtown toward the Pearl, Darren realizes he could simply forego the tip—after all, it's on account, and not very much.

But forgoing the tip also means losing face, and if Yukio ever finds out who he is, then he'll never live this down—not that he could live it down anyway. His days as Quizmo of Portland would be over; everyone would laugh at a seemingly all-powerful man with a brilliant mind who rides a bicycle for a living.

He tries not to think about the upcoming encounter. He tucks the package in his bag and hurries across the streets. In Portland, drivers obey the rules of the road, so he takes advantage of red lights, stop signs and polite drivers stopping for pedestrians.

He makes it across the downtown in less than five minutes. When he reaches the outside of the Hanley, Hanley, Combs and Whitmore building, he padlocks his bike illegally to a parking meter, grabs the package and heads for the door.

Yukio isn't there. The doorman is a middle-aged man whom Darren hasn't seen before. When the doorman offers to take the package upstairs, Darren lets him, willing to lose the tip to add a few more minutes to his weekend.

All he has to do is ride back to headquarters, drop off his bike bag and his payment log, and then head home. He has the entire weekend ahead of him—no bars host quiz programs on Fridays or Saturdays; he doesn't have to be back to work until 9 p.m. on Sunday night and then at the easiest bar on his list.

He unlocks the bike and sees a movement near the alleyway. Yukio, in his doorman's blues, tosses a still-burning cigarette into the gutter.

Darren fumbles with the lock, his fingers suddenly shaking. He has to focus on the combination; for a brief moment, he cannot remember it.

When he finally snaps the lock open, he looks up. Yukio has gone back inside.

Darren hates that one of his players is on his regular route. It'd be so easy for the player to out him, and a player like Yukio, who can't take responsibility for his own losses, is the very sort of man who would do so.

Darren rides back to headquarters so distracted that he nearly rear-ends a Volkswagen stopped at the light near Waterfront Park.

On the way home, he picks up a six-pack of Budweiser but forgets to stop at the video store. He's stuck with *O Brother Where Art Thou*, which he has already seen twice.

He watches it again that night, then follows it with the director's commentary. He listens to the music, looks at the trailer, wonders if George Clooney is too thin, if the Coen Brothers are as whacked as they seem. Over the course of the weekend—a weekend that he had planned to spend in Portland State University's library, looking up information in newly minted doctoral theses—he sees *O Brother* a total of five times (the director's commentary three times, which really takes his total to eight times).

By Sunday night, he's so woozy he considers taking 1930s bluegrass out of the pop culture category and putting it in the general category. Then he realizes his mistake. He's not sure he can handle a quiz crowd, even a quiz crowd at Buster's Bar and Rodeo.

Still, he shows up. He hasn't missed a night at any of his bars, not even when he had the Martian death flu two winters back—the kind that had him yacking every fifteen minutes or so into a bucket beside announcer's booth.

He goes and he works, ignoring the screams from the mechanical bull riders two rooms over, glad that this crowd muffs most of the questions while trying to answer them because that means the contest ends quicker.

But somewhere around round three, he realizes that one team is getting its questions. He squints through DVD-blurred eyes and sees a woman with a purple kerchief, worn babushka style. She's toward the back and she's not ringing in, but she's supplying answers to her team—the Great American Cowgirls.

He's half tempted to get off the chair behind the dance platform, leaving the mike off, and get a drink, just so that he can see if she's as square as he remembered, her arms as thick, and her breasts as saggy.

But he shakes himself free of the impulse and continues as if she's not there at all. While he plays half of Billy Ray Cyrus's only platinum album during the break after Round Five (Billy Ray in quantity is guaranteed to piss off any good country loving crowd), he pads the Impossible Round with as many esoteric math questions as he can get away with, much more esoteric than the math questions that stumped Cindy at the Triangle.

He starts the round just as the crowd gets surly, and for the first time, he wonders if he's lost them. A woman down front starts screaming for Alan Jackson until someone shuts her up, reminding her that Request Night isn't until Tuesday. One good ole boy punches another near the bar, and the bar back, a former high school linebacker nicknamed Dumbbell (for both his weight and his IQ), drags both men out by their ears so that the punches don't turn into an out-and-out brawl.

This Impossible Round matches Round Four at the Triangle in degrees of difficulty. Sure enough, Cindy—or the woman who looks stunningly like her—manages to answer the first ten questions covering everything from astronomy to microbiology to the development of the pillow book in premodern Japanese literature.

But she misses the math questions. All of them. And that oversight brings the only remaining competitive team—the Beer Goggles—into first place. They win a gift certificate for Powell's Books, some free beers that they don't need, and five rides on the mechanical bull as well as a little computerized award sheet that looks oddly like a diploma that the manager of the bar insists on making up after each Sunday night competition.

By the time Darren finishes his announcements on the prizes, Cindy—or her look-alike—is gone, vanished into the crowd or off to try her luck on the mechanical bull.

Darren feels oddly relieved. He doesn't want to think about her.

He doesn't want to think about anything except tomorrow's quiz.

Darren packs up his gear and slides his laptop under his arm, walking out to his piece-of-crap car (no bike on quiz nights) before remembering that he hasn't gone to the bar manager for his check and his cut of the night's proceedings.

He gets woozy sometimes, and he's gone into the job sick, but never before has he forgotten to pick up his check. He's still not on his A game.

***

FOR THE NEXT TWO DAYS, he manages to avoid deliveries to Hanley, Hanley, Combs and Whitmore. He conducts his quizzes, stocking his Impossible Rounds with math questions because he feels like he's being stalked by Cindy the Trivia Wonder Creature.

Finally, on Wednesday, he can't avoid another trip to Hanley. Yukio is there, cupping an unlit cigarette in his hand as Darren locks his bike to the nearest parking meter.

"You can't park there," Yukio says.

"I can't park anywhere else either," Darren snaps. "You people won't guard it for me."

He puts a nasty emphasis on *you people* that surprises even himself. Yukio frowns at him, and Darren's breath catches. In that biting sentence, Yukio probably heard the voice of Quizmo. Yukio probably recognized it.

Yukio puts one hand on his hip, tilts his head, and says, "You're that bike messenger who snuck in here last week."

Darren's relieved. Yukio has recognized him, but not as Quizmo.

"I didn't sneak," Darren says. "I was doing my job. I showed you my identification."

And then because he must retain his power in this relationship, Darren stalks into the building.

The second doorman, the middle-aged loser, reaches for the package, but Darren doesn't give it to him. Even though he will only get a seven-dollar tip, even though he will lose time on his next (and bigger paying) job, he must do this. He must show Yukio who is in charge.

His cleats click on the marble. The package is clammy beneath his arm, probably from his own sweat. He watches reflections in the mirrored glass of the elevator, hoping for Yukio, but Yukio doesn't come after him.

As he puts the package in the hand of the Birkenstocked receptionist and takes his paltry signed form, indicating his tiny tip, he realizes just how petty he's become, playing games no one else participates in, games no one else even knows are going on.

He feels, for the first time in his aimless life, as if he's trapped in a Coen Brothers' movie, and he has no idea how to get out.

***

THE BRAINIACS ALWAYS SHOW UP early at Buzzard Bill's on Wednesday night. They eat dinner together, have a beer or two, and relax before the quizzing starts.

As Darren sets up, he stares at their table. Yukio is there, wearing a faded blue shirt over ripped jeans. He seems shorter, squatter, than he does in his uniform—and not as exotic.

Yukio clutches a book—*Great Minds' Trivia Challenge*—something Darren only used in his first year of quizzing and has since moved beyond, preferring to draw up his own questions.

Something niggles at him, something he's missed in his assumptions, something that has bothered him from the start. Darren sets his sheets out for the first round as the door opens. In Buzzard Bill's, the mike stand is only a few feet from the door and early in the evening—particularly in the summer—he gets blinded whenever the light shines in.

It is no different now. But as the door eases closed, he sees the scarf first—this one a loud yellow and green—and then the rest of her, done up in green pants with a yellow blouse, and weird yellow sandals.

She grins at him, and he feels surprise. She has tracked him down. For a week—maybe more—she has followed him from bar to bar, playing the quizzes and doing better than most.

But for the math questions…

Math questions Yukio usually aces.

Darren's frown grows deeper. She walks across the bar floor after waving three fingers of her right hand at him and then slides into the booth beside Yukio.

There is a resemblance, the resemblance of siblings or cousins, the kind that leaves no doubt that these two people have sprung from the same gene pool.

Darren's stomach flops over. Is Cindy somehow involved in Yukio's obsession or is she just humoring him?

I heard it was hard, she'd said to Darren that first night. Heard from Yukio? Was she practicing? Scouting? Or trying to show Yukio up?

In the end, Darren decides it's none of his business. He's going to do what he always does: He's going to put on the best quiz show possible for everyone involved.

It isn't until the middle of the first round that he realizes he's in trouble.

Cindy has joined the Brainiacs, bringing their number to the requisite six. Technically, that wouldn't be a problem except that she can answer every question he throws at them.

Except the math questions.

Which he has loaded heavily into the last three rounds.

Math questions Yukio can answer in his sleep.

Quizmo will no longer be all knowing, the great god of information, champion of the geek Olympics, smartest man in the room.

He will become worse than his losers—a man who can be beaten at his own game.

He will become, in the space of an evening, absolutely nothing.

***

By the end of Round Two, he knows he must find other questions, new subjects, some way to defeat the juggernaut that is Yukio and his sister.

Darren knows that Cindy is Yukio's sister because one of the Brainiacs hits on her, and Yukio looms over him, warning the would-be Lothario to leave his sister alone.

At the end of round three, Darren has exhausted his laptop's deep files—all the information he's hidden over the years of running quizzes has risen to the surface, and is now part of the game.

He cannot use any questions from earlier in the week, because Cindy has participated in every round.

He is stuck, and he knows it.

Sweat breaks out on his forehead. His fingertips are slick with condensation from his glass of water mixed with the weird stuff that coats Goldfish crackers. He's been eating those by the handful, trying to calm himself. All he's managed to do is turn his hands yellow and make his stomach feel like mush.

As he heads for the men's restroom in the now-closed restaurant, a hand grabs his arm. He recognizes the grip. It hits the same bruises that formed a week ago, after Yukio tried to stop him from getting into the Hanley, Hanley, Combs and Whitmore building.

"We're going to beat you," Yukio says. "We're going to leave your brain battered and bloody, exposed for all to see."

Then he releases Darren's arm and it is all Darren can do to keep from rubbing the newly aggravated bruises. He staggers into the private section of the restaurant, where only employees can go after ten p.m., and disappears into the men's room. He almost shoves the large metal garbage can against the door, but decides against it. All that will do is show his own fear.

Why does Yukio hate him so? What has he done, really? All he's been doing is running a little game.

At least Yukio still doesn't recognize him.

Yet in both places – in the bars and at the Hanley building—they have ended up in pissing contests, and so far, Darren has won.

At the thought of pissing, his bladder reminds him of the reason for his trip across the bar. He heads to the urinal, braces himself with one hand against the spotless wall because he's still a little too shaky to remain upright, and relieves himself.

Threats of violence usually didn't shake him. He's small but he's tough thanks to all those years of cycling. But that image—his brain bloody, battered and exposed—won't leave him.

He washes his hands, splashes water on his face, and peers at himself in the mirror. The Brainiacs are going to beat him—Yukio and Cindy are going to beat him.

He doesn't know how to stop them.

He makes himself breathe. It's one night. One night of one game. It's not as if he's going to lose his entire empire.

Except that Cindy has scoped out every bar, learned the names of his favorite teams in all of his weekly haunts. If she and Yukio defeat him here, they can—and perhaps will—defeat him everywhere.

He doesn't know what to do.

But he knows he has to do something.

***

BY THE END OF ROUND FIVE, Yukio is smirking. Cindy isn't even pretending to be a part of the Brainiacs' backup team. She buzzes in quicker than anyone else, even her brother.

The other teams have already been eliminated, and so there is no need for the Impossible Round.

The crowd is getting surly. They want to see a competition, not one team crushing another. Darren's asked all his most difficult questions, wasting years of the Truly Impossible File on a single game. He can't even go back to the questions from earlier in the week because Cindy has heard them all.

Still, he leans into the mike and says, "Believe it or not, folks, we are going to have an Impossible Round. It'll just take a moment to get it organized."

He is so angry that he puts Olivia Newton John's last album on the sound system, forcing the crowd to listen to whining songs about inappropriate lovers while he tries to come up with a solution.

Yukio and Cindy are laughing with the Brainiacs. The other teams have crowded the bar, demanding even more alcohol. For Buzzard Bill's, the night is still good.

It's only going badly for Darren.

Cindy looks up, grins at Darren and then winks, as if they share a secret. She takes the ugly scarf off her hair, and he finally understands why she wore it. Without it, her resemblance to her brother is startling.

Darren clenches his fist. Yukio and Cindy have made a point to know all sorts of esoteric information about all sorts of things. They have minds that capture inane facts and save them for no apparent reason. They're smart people with unsmart jobs—at least in the case of Yukio—and they probably wonder, deep down, why they aren't running the world.

In short, they're like him.

But they're not like him. A doorman has no practical function. He's not a janitor or a plumber, someone with hands-on skill. All a doorman has to do is scrutinize people who come and go from a building. And when Darren confronted Yukio, even though Yukio got physical, he backed down.

"You gonna shut that crap off soon?" The cocktail waitress stands behind him. She sets down a bottled water and a glass of ice, just like he requested at the beginning of the night. And another bowl of Goldfish crackers. "I never liked this stuff when it was popular twenty years ago."

"Me, either," Darren says.

"So do something, would you?" She makes a face at him, as if he's the most stupid person on earth, and then she wades back into the crowd.

Do something.

Of course. That's the problem with Brainiacs. People who spend all their time learning useless facts have no practical side. That's what he's been groping for, that's what he needs.

He has to ask questions smart people will miss—simple questions, questions that are about practical things. Yet they have to seem esoteric.

If only he can think of questions like that.

He turns the sound down on that horrible music, then grabs the mike so hard that feedback echoes through the bar.

The crowd grows instantly silent.

"The Brainiacs win tonight's prize," he says—and there's a groan from the other teams, who somehow hoped for a lightning elimination round or something— "but we have an extra special prize, a once-in-a-lifetime prize, that goes to the winner of the Impossible Round."

He has the crowd now. They're staring at him.

His heart pounds as if he's pedaled all across Portland. If he screws this up, he's done.

"Since we all know that the Brainiacs won because of their two team members, Yukio and Cindy, who answered every one of tonight's questions, I'm making the Impossible Round their round. *Only* Yukio or Cindy may answer a question. No one may help them. The rest of you Brainiacs, get yourselves a beer and absent yourselves from the team table. If anyone helps Yukio or Cindy, they forfeit and their team forfeits—"

"What if someone from another team helps?" a Brainiac shouts, clearly worried.

"Then the team's barred from the game here at Buzzard Bill's."

The bartender looks up in panic. Darren isn't authorized to make these kinds of rules or those kinds of decisions. He hopes it won't come to that.

"Ten questions," he says, "with ten subheadings."

"Do they get the special prize or do all the Brainiacs?" another Brainiac shouts.

He makes a quick decision. "You all do. Yukio and Cindy are playing for the whole team."

The Brainiacs cross their arms, but they move away from the team table. Suddenly Yukio and Cindy are in the spotlight, and for the first time that night, they look nervous.

"Yukio and Cindy, are you ready?" Darren asks.

"Sure," Yukio says, his bravado back.

Darren clears his throat, takes a deep breath, and asks, "Question One: What is the albedo of the earth, in aggregate?"

"I'll take that." Cindy grins at her brother. He shrugs. She presses her handheld buzzer, then says, "It's zero-point-three."

"Subquestion A," Darren says, "How is the albedo calculated?"

"Oh, shit," Cindy says without hitting the buzzer. "Who really cares?"

"I do," Yukio says. He buzzes in. "If you have a spec-toradiometer and you face it toward the sun…"

Darren listens but he doesn't really hear. He pays just enough attention to know that they are getting each question and the following subquestions. And as he suspected, Yukio takes the math questions while Cindy handles all the rest.

She destroys the history section. And the literature section. Finally, Darren gets to his most esoteric question, the one he doubts even a collector or an antique dealer can answer.

"What is…" he asks slowly "…a Caron Derringer?"

Yukio hits the buzzer. "It's a gun manufactured in—"

"It's a perfume atomizer," Cindy says over the top of him. Darren's stomach does a flip-flop.

"Yukio buzzed in," Darren says. "He has to give the complete answer."

She turns to her brother, whispers to him.

Darren bangs a hand on the counter, making the mike reverberate. "Yukio has to answer on his own."

"We're playing as a team," she says. "Team members can consult."

Darren supposes he can challenge that. They're playing as a truncated team. He can disqualify this question, and make sure they don't work together again.

But he doesn't want to defeat them by default. He wants the win to be fair and square, so that no one, particularly not Yukio, can say he cheated.

"Okay," Darren says. "Yukio, give me the answer."

"It's a perfume atomizer marketed in 1963 under the Caron brand. It's so small it can fit into a purse or a lipstick case. It doesn't look like a derringer, but rather like a derringer's bullet."

Complete, accurate, and devastating. A question like that would demolish even the better-than-average player. Cindy isn't better than average. She's the best Darren's seen. Her math weakness is her only flaw.

Darren's hands continue to shake. He's not sure he can keep up this game much longer. His head is throbbing and he feels slightly woozy. If she can answer the Caron Derringer question, she can answer almost anything. And his own math skills aren't great enough to take on Yukio—at least not on the highest levels.

He hasn't thought of any real world questions, not any he's sure of the answers to. He doesn't know much about plumbing or construction either.

But he does know biking. Only, if he asks a bicycle question, will Yukio realize that the Great Quizmo is really a lowly bike messenger?

Yukio is staring at him. So is the rest of the bar, waiting for the next question.

Either Yukio and Cindy defeat him here, defeat him now, or Yukio defeats him later—should he recognize Darren.

The risk is Darren's.

And he takes it.

He says, "In cycling, what was Kryptonite's kryptonite?"

The entire bar gasps. The Kryptonite lock, the best of all bike locks, supposedly undefeatable, impossible to break into, turned out to be easily opened with a ballpoint pen. Because Portland has such a large cycling community, the story made front-page news in the *Oregonian* a few years ago. The company that makes Kryptonite fixed the flaw immediately and offered every cyclist who had purchased a Kryptonite lock a replacement.

Yukio is looking down. Cindy frowns. Around them, people squirm in their chairs. A few of the Brainiacs, sitting as far from the competitors' tables as possible, whisper to each other, obviously shocked at their teammates' silence.

The whole bar knows the answer.

"It was in the paper," Yukio says without buzzing in. "I saw it."

Cindy studies him as if she can will the answer out of him.

"Something picks that lock," Yukio says.

Cindy remains quiet.

Yukio turns toward the bar, but Darren clears his throat into the microphone. No one says anything, even though a few people clearly want to.

Then Yukio looks at Cindy, who shrugs.

"Your first four minutes are nearly up," Darren says. He wonders if he can live with himself if he sets the final minute timer at thirty seconds.

But he doesn't have to cheat. Instead, Yukio buzzes in. "It's a paperclip!"

The entire bar groans. Darren allows himself a small triumphant smile, then leans toward the mike. "You people want to tell him what he did wrong?"

In unison, the patrons shout, "A ballpoint pen!"

Yukio looks stunned, Cindy confused.

Darren's heart is still pounding, but the pounding comes from an unfamiliar elation. He's never felt like this—at least not in quizzing. Once or twice when he's had to beat the clock messengering, he's hit a biker's high. That's what this feels like. The quizmaster's high.

"And that's it for tonight's game. If you losers are still feeling confident, come back for next week's tournament, and see whose brain ends up bloody, battered, and exposed for the weak muscle that it is. Until then, this is Quizmo, reminding you all that my mind is greater than yours."

Yukio cringes, but looks defeated. He doesn't seem like a man who has recognized a bike messenger. He seems like a man whose brain has been exposed.

If Yukio was going to do anything, he would have done it the moment he lost the question.

But he didn't.

Darren's won. He wants to jump with his arms overhead like a football player who has just made a touchdown.

Instead, he settles for blaring Queen's "We are the Champions" over the sound system.

Yukio's teammates have surrounded his table, battering him with questions—*How could he miss that? It was so easy.* Darren smiles. Yukio looks lost, clearly wondering why one missed easy question destroys his entire reputation as a brainiac.

Because, Darren can tell him but won't, *the easy questions show the posturers for the real-life losers that they are.*

"My brother thought he could beat you." Cindy's standing near the back of the mike stand. Darren looks for the cocktail waitress, the bouncer, someone in authority to tell Cindy to move out of the way, but they're busy.

He's alone.

"No one beats the amazing Quizmo," Darren says, but there isn't as much heart in the words as there was a few minutes ago.

She gives him a saucy grin. "I'd like to."

It takes him a minute to realize she's making a double entendre. Then it takes another minute to realize she's serious. He blushes so deeply that the heat in his face actually hurts.

Her dark eyes meet his. He studies her for a moment. He's beginning to get used to her exotic look and he's starting to think she's handsome in a way that only improves with age.

Her mind is compatible with his—right down to the level of trivial interests and her inability to go to higher levels in math. If he says yes, he could be with her for a very long time. They'd be perfect together—the kind of couple who would build a geeky life in this geeky town.

He'd quit quizzing and take a job at Intel or one of the other remaining high tech firms. She'd continue doing whatever it is that keeps her in beer and potato chips.

Together they'd have two scarily brilliant children, a few cats, and a house in the West Hills. Eventually, he'd gain weight because he can't cycle any more, and he'd start frequenting bars like this one just once a week, coming for the "entertainment" and not for the escape, wondering what it would've been like if he'd continued in his quest for fame.

He would never know, but he would fantasize about it, like all of these people here, people who leave every week and go back to their average lives in their average houses with their average spouses.

He can't believe he's thinking of dating her. He can't believe he's thinking of sleeping with her.

For a moment—just a brief moment—he forgot he is the Amazing Quizmo, Master of All He Sees.

"Sorry," he says to Cindy as he pushes past her, "but the only person who can beat me is myself."

Patriotic Gestures

*P*AMELA KINNEY HEARD THE NOISE in her sleep—giggles, followed by the crunching of leaves. Later, she smelled smoke, faint and acrid, and realized that her neighbors were burning garbage in their fireplace again. She got up long enough to close the window and silently curse them; she hated it when they did illegal burning.

She forgot about it until the next morning. She stepped out her back door into the crisp fall morning, and found charred remains of her flag in the middle of her driveway. There'd been no wind during the night, fortunately, or all the evidence would have been gone.

Instead, there was a pile of burned fabric and a burn stain on the pavement. There were even footprints outlined in leaves.

She noted all of that with a professional's detachment—she'd eyeballed more than a thousand crime scenes—before the fabric itself caught her attention. Then the pain was sudden and swift, right above her heart, echoing through the breastbone and down her back.

Anyone else would have thought she was having a heart attack. But she wasn't, and she knew it. She'd had this feeling twice before, first when the officers came to her house and then when the chaplain handed her the folded flag which just a moment before had draped over her daughter's coffin.

Pamela had clung to that flag like she'd seen so many other military mothers do, and she suspected she had looked as lost as they had. Then, when she stood, that pain ran through her, dropping her back to the chair.

Her sons took her arms, and when she mentioned the pain, they dragged her to the emergency room. She had been late for her own daughter's wake, her chest sticky with adhesive from the cardiac machines and her hair smelling faintly of disinfectant.

And the feeling came back now, as she stared at the massacre before her. The flag, Jenny's flag, had been ripped from the front door and burned in her driveway.

Pamela made herself breathe. Then she rubbed that spot above her left breast, felt the pain spread through-out her body, burning her eyes and forming a lump in the back of her throat. But she held the tears back. She wouldn't give whoever had done this awful thing the sat-isfaction.

Finally she reached inside her purse for her cell, called Neil—she had trouble thinking of him as the sheriff after all the years she'd known him— and then she protected the scene until he arrived.

***

IT ONLY TOOK HIM FIVE MINUTES. Halleysburg was still a small town, no matter how many Portlanders sprawled into the community, willing to make the one and a half hour one-way daily commute to the city's edge. Pamela had told the dispatch to make sure that Neil parked across the street so that any wind from his vehicle wouldn't move the leaves.

And she had asked for a second scene-of-the-crime kit because she didn't want to go inside and get hers. She didn't want to risk losing the crime scene with a moment of inattention.

Neil pulled onto the street. His car was an unwieldy Olds with a souped up engine and a reinforced frame. It could take a lot of punishment, and often did.

As a result, the paint covering the car's sides was fresh and clean, while the hood, roof and trunk looked like they were covered in dirt.

The sheriff was the same. Neil Karlyn was in his late fifties, balding, with a face that had seen too much sun. But his uniform was always new, always pristine, and never wrinkled. He'd been that way since college, a precise man with precise opinions about a difficult world.

He got out of the Olds and did not reach around back for a scene-of-the-crime kit. Annoyance threaded through her.

"Where's my kit?" she asked.

"Pam," he said gently, "it's a low-level property crime. It'll never go to trial and you know it."

"It's arson with malicious intent," she snapped. "That's a felony."

He sighed and studied her for a moment. He clearly recognized her tone. She'd used it often enough on him when they were students at the University of Oregon. When they were lovers on different sides of the political fence, and constantly on the verge of splitting up.

When they finally did, it had taken years for them to settle into a friendship. But settle they did. They hardly even fought any more.

He went back to the car, opened the back seat and removed the kit she'd requested. She crossed her arms, waiting as he walked toward her. He stopped at the edge of the curb, holding the kit tight against his leg.

"Even if you somehow get the D.A. to agree that this is a cockamamie felony, you know that processing the scene yourself taints the evidence."

"Why do you care so much?" she asked, hearing an edge in her voice that usually wasn't there. The challenge, unspoken: *It's my daughter's flag. It's like murdering her all over again.*

To his credit, Neil didn't try to soothe her with a platitude.

"It's the eighth flag this morning," he said. "It's not personal, Pam."

Her chin jutted out. "It is to me."

Neil looked down, his cheek moving. He was clenching his jaw, trying not to speak.

He didn't have to.

She understood the irony of the statement. Somewhere in her pile of college paraphernalia was a badly framed newspaper clipping that had once been the front page of the Portland *Oregonian*. She'd framed the clipping so that a photo dominated, a photo of a much-younger Pamela with long hair and a tie-dye t-shirt, front and center in a group of students, holding an American flag by a stick, watching as it burned.

God, she could still remember how that felt, to hold a flag up so that the wind caught it. How fabric had its own acrid odor, and how frightened she'd been at the desecration, even though she'd been the one to light the flag on fire.

She had been protesting the Vietnam War. It was that photo and the resulting brouhaha it caused, both on campus and in the State of Oregon itself, that had led to the final break-up with Neil.

He couldn't believe what she had done. Sometimes she couldn't either. But she felt her country was worth fighting for. So had he. He joined up not two months later.

To his credit, Neil didn't say anything about her own flag-burning as he handed her the kit. Instead he watched as she took photographs of the scene, scooped up the charred bits of fabric, and made a sketch of the footprint she found in the leaves.

She found another print in the yard, and that one she made a cast of. Then she dusted her front door for prints, trying not to cry as she did so.

"A flag is a flag is a flag," she used to say.

Until it draped over her daughter's coffin.

Until it became all she had left.

***

"I CALLED THE LOCAL VFW, MOM," her son Stephen said over dinner that night. Stephen was her oldest and had been her support for thirty years, since the day his father walked out, never to return. "They're bringing another flag."

She stirred the mashed potatoes into the creamed corn on her plate. The meal had come from KFC: her sons had brought a bucket with her favorite sides, and told her not to argue with them about the fast food meal.

She wasn't arguing, but she didn't have much of an appetite.

They sat in the dining room, at the table that had once held four of them. Pamela had slid the fake rose centerpiece in front of Jenny's place, so she wouldn't have to think about her daughter.

It wasn't working.

"Another flag isn't the same, dumbass," Travis said. At thirty, he was the youngest, unmarried, still finding himself, a phrase she had come to hate.

The hell of it was, Travis was right. It wasn't the same. That flag these people had burned, that flag had comforted her. She had clung to it on the worst afternoon of her life, her fingers holding it tight, even at the emergency room, when the doctors wanted to pry it from her hands.

It had taken almost a week for her to let it go. Stephen had come over, Stephen and his pretty wife Elaine and their teenage daughters, Mandy and Liv. They'd brought KFC then, too, and talked about everything but the war.

Until it came time to take the flag away from Pamela.

Stephen had talked to her like she was a five-year-old who wanted to take her blankie to kindergarten. In the end, she'd handed the flag over. He'd been the one to find the old flagpole, the one she'd taken down when she bought the house, and he'd been the one to place the pole in the hanger outside the front door.

"The VFW says they replace flags all the time," Stephen said to his brother.

"Because some idiot burned one?" Travis asked.

Pamela's cheeks flushed.

"Because people lose them. Or moths eat them. Or sometimes, they get stolen," Stephen said.

"But not burned," Travis persisted.

Pamela swallowed. Travis didn't remember the newspaper photo, but Stephen probably did. It had hung over the console stereo she had gotten when her mother died, and it had been a teacher—Neil's first grade teacher? Pamela couldn't remember—who had seen it at a party and asked if she really wanted her children to see that before they could understand what it meant.

"I don't want another one," Pamela said.

"Mom…." Stephen started in his most reasonable voice.

She shook her head. "It's been a year. I need to move on."

"You don't move on from that kind of loss," Travis said, and she wondered how he knew. He didn't have children.

Then she looked at him, a large broad-shouldered man with tears in his eyes, and remembered that Jenny had been the one who walked him to school, who bathed him at night, who usually tucked him in. Jenny had done all that because Stephen at thirteen was already working to help his mom make ends meet, and Pamela was working two jobs herself, as well as attending community college to get her degree in forensic science and criminology. A pseudoscience degree, one of her almost-boyfriends had said. But it wasn't. She used science every day. She needed science like she needed air.

Like she needed to find out who had destroyed her daughter's flag.

"You don't move on," Pamela said.

Her boys watched her. Sometimes she could see the babies they had been in the lines of their mouths and the shape of their eyes. She still marveled at the way they had grown into men, large men who could carry her the way she used to carry them.

"But," she added, "you don't have to dwell on it, every moment of every day."

And yet she was dwelling. She couldn't stop. She never told her sons or anyone else, not even Neil who had become a closer friend in the year since Jenny had died. Neil, a widower now, a man who understood death the way that Pamela did. Neil, whose grandson had enlisted after 9/11 and had somehow made it back.

She was dwelling and there was only one way to stop. She had to use science to solve this. She couldn't think about it emotionally. She had to think about it clinically.

She had her evidence and she needed even more.

The next morning, the local paper ran an article on the burnings, and listed the addresses in the police log section. So Pamela visited the other crime scenes with her kit and her camera, identifying herself as an employee of the State Crime Lab.

Since *CSI* debuted on television, that identification opened doors for her. She didn't have to tell the other victims that she had been a victim too.

She took pictures of scorch marks on pavement and flag holders wrenched loose of their sockets. She removed flag bits from garbage cans, and studied footprints in the leaf-covered grass to see if they looked similar to the ones on her lawn.

And late that afternoon, as she stepped back to photograph yet another twisted flag holder beside a front door, she saw the glint of a camera hiding in a cobwebby corner of the door frame. The house was a starter, maybe 1200 square feet total. She wouldn't have expected a camera here.

"Do you have a security system?" she asked the homeowner, a woman Travis's age who looked like she hadn't slept in weeks. Her name was Becky something. Pamela hadn't really heard her last name in the introduction.

"My husband put it up," Becky said, her voice shaking a little. "I have no idea how it works."

"When will he be back?" Pamela asked.

Becky shrugged. "When they cancel stop-loss, I guess."

Pamela felt her breath slide out of her body. "He's in Iraq?"

Becky nodded. "I put the flag up for him, you know? And I haven't told him what happened to it. I've gotta find someone to fix the holder, and I have to get another flag."

Pamela looked at the house more closely. It needed paint. The bushes in front were overgrown. There were cobwebs all over the windows, and dry rot on the sills. Obviously the couple had purchased it expecting someone to work on it.

Either the money wasn't there, or the husband had planned to do the work himself.

"I can fix the holder," Pamela said. "If you have a few tools."

"My husband does," Becky said. "I can show them to you."

"I have a few things to finish, and then you can show me," Pamela said.

She dusted for prints, and then, for comparison, took Becky's and some off the husband's comb, which hadn't been touched since he left. Then Pamela went into his workroom, which also hadn't been touched, and took a hammer, some screws, and a screwdriver.

It took only ten minutes to repair the flag holder. But in that time, she'd made a friend.

"How'd you learn how to do that?" Becky asked.

"Raised three kids alone," Pamela said. "You realize there's not much you can't do, if you just try."

Becky nodded.

Pamela glanced at the camera. Untended since the husband left. It was probably in the same state of disrepair as the rest of the house.

"Can I see the security system?" she asked.

"It's not really a system," Becky said. "Just the cameras, and some motion sensors that're supposed to alert us when someone's on the property. But they clearly don't work any more."

"Let me see anyway," Pamela said.

Becky took her past the workroom, into a small closet filled with electronics. The closet was warm from the heat the panels gave off. Lights still blinked.

Pamela stared at it all, then touched the rewind button on the digital recorder. On the television monitor, she watched an image of herself fixing the flag holder.

"It looks like the camera's still working," she said. "Mind if I rewind farther?"

"Go ahead."

Backwards, she watched darkness turn to day. Saw Neil inspect the hanger. Saw Becky crying, then the tears evaporate into a stare of disbelief before she backed off the porch and away from the scene.

Back to the previous night. No porch light. Just images blurred in the darkness. Faces, not quite real, mostly turned away from the camera.

"Got a recordable DVD?" Pamela asked.

"Somewhere." Becky vanished into the house. Pamela studied the system, hoping that she wouldn't erase the information as she tried to record it.

She rewound again. Studied the faces, the half turned heads. She saw crew cuts and piercings and hoodies. Slouchy clothes worn by half the young people in Halleysburg.

Nothing to identify them. Nothing to separate them from everyone else in their age group.

Like her, her hair long, her jeans torn, as she stood front and center at the U of O, a burning flag before her.

She made herself study the machine, and figured out how to save the images to the disk's hard drive so that they wouldn't be erased. Then she inspected the buttons near the machine's DVD slot.

"Here," Becky said, thrusting a packet at her.

DVD-Rs, unopened, dust-covered. Pamela used a fingernail to break the seal, then pulled one out, and inserted it in the slot. She managed to record, but had no way to test. So she made a few more copies, feeling somewhat reassured that she could come back and try to download the images from the hard drive again.

"Will this catch them?" Becky asked while she watched the process.

"I don't know," Pamela said. "I hope so."

"It's just, they got so close, you know." Becky's voice shook. "I didn't know anyone could get that close."

It took Pamela a moment to understand what she meant. Becky meant that they had gotten close to the house. Close to her. The burning hadn't just upset her, it had frightened her, and made her feel vulnerable.

Odd. All it had done to Pamela was make her angry.

"Just lock up at night," Pamela said after a minute. "Locks deter ninety-percent of all thieves."

"And the remaining ten percent?"

They get in, Pamela almost said, but thought the better of it.

"They don't usually come to places like Halleysburg," she said. "Why would they? We all know each other here."

Becky nodded, seemingly reassured. Or maybe she just wanted to abandon an uncomfortable topic.

Pamela certainly did. She wanted to play with the images, see what she could find.

She wanted a solid image of the culprits, one that she could bring to Neil.

Maybe then, he would stop complaining that this was a petty property crime. Maybe then he might understand how important this really was.

***

But it was her own words that replayed in her head later that night as she sat in front of her computer.

They don't usually come to places like Halleysburg.... We all know each other here.

She had lied to make Becky feel better, but the words hadn't felt like a lie. Thieves really didn't come here.

There was no need. There was richer pickings in Portland or Salem or the nearby bedroom communities.

Besides, it was hard to commit a crime here without someone seeing you.

Except under cover of darkness.

Her home office was quiet. It overlooked the back yard, and she had never installed curtains on the window, preferring the view of the year-round flower garden she had planted. At the moment, her garden was full of browns and oranges, fall plants blooming despite the winter ahead. She had little lights beneath the plants, lights she usually kept off because they spiked her energy bill.

But she had them on now. She would probably have them on for some time to come.

Maybe Becky wasn't the only one who felt vulnerable.

Pamela put one of the DVDs in her computer, and opened the images. They played, much to her relief, so she copied the images to her hard drive and removed the DVD.

Her computer at home wasn't as good as her computer at work. But it would have to do.

She didn't want to do any work on this case at the State Crime Lab if she could help it. The lab was so understaffed and so overworked that it usually took four months to get something tested. When she last checked, more than 600 cases were backlogged, some of them dating back more than nine months.

Those cases were bigger than hers. The backlogs were semen samples from possible rapists and blood droplets from the scene of a multiple murder case.

She couldn't, in good conscience, bring something personal and private to the lab. She would work here as long as she could. Then if she couldn't finish here, she might be able to convince herself that the time she took at the lab would go toward an arson case—a serious one, not a petty property crime, as Neil had called it.

Petty property crime.

Funny that they would be on opposite sides of this issue too.

Pamela went through the images frame by frame, looking for clear faces. Her computer didn't have the face recognition software that one of the computers at the lab had, but she had installed a home version of image sharpening software. She used it to clean out the fuzz and to lighten the darkness, trying to find more than a chin or the corner of an ear.

Finally she got a small face just behind the flag, a serious white face with a frown—of disapproval? She couldn't tell—and a bit of an elongated chin. Enough to see the wisp of a beard—a boy's beard, more a wish of a beard than the real thing—and a tattooed hand coming up to catch the flag as the person almost blocking the camera yanked the pole out of the holder.

She blew up the image, softened it, fixed it, and then felt tears prick her eyes.

They don't usually come to places like Halleysburg.

No. They grew up here. And worked at the grocery store down the street to pay for their football uniforms at the underfunded high school. They collected coins in a can on Sunday afternoons for Boosters, and they smiled when they saw her and respectfully called her Mrs. Kinney and asked, with a little too much interest, how her granddaughters were doing.

"Jeremy Stallings," she whispered. "What the hell were you thinking?"

And she hoped she knew.

***

NEIL WOULDN'T LET HER SIT IN while he questioned Jeremy Stallings. He was appalled she'd even asked.

"That sort of thing belongs on TV and you know it," he'd said.

But she also knew he probably wouldn't do much more than slap the boy on the wrist, so what would be the harm? She hadn't made that argument, though.

Instead, she waited on the bench chair outside the sheriff's office conference room, which doubled as an interview room on days like this, and watched the parade of parents and lawyers as they trooped past.

No one acknowledged her. No one so much as looked at her. Not Reg Stallings, whose brother had sold her the house, or his wife June, who had taken over the PTA just before Travis got out of high school. No one mentioned the friendly exchanges at the high school football games or the hellos at the diner behind the movie theater. It was easier to forget all that and pretend they weren't neighbors than it was to acknowledge what was going on inside that room.

Then, finally, Jeremy came out. He was wearing his baggy pants with a Halo t-shirt hanging nearly to his knees. He wore that same frown he'd had as he took the flag off from Becky's front door.

He glanced at Pamela, then looked away, a blush working its way up the spider tattoo on his neck into his crew cut.

His parents and the lawyers led him away, as Neil reminded all of them to be in court the following morning.

Neil waited until they went through the front doors before coming over to Pamela.

She stood, her knees creaky from sitting so long. "He confess?"

Neil nodded. "And gave me the names of his buddies."

Pamela bit her lower lip. "Funny," she said, "he didn't strike me as the type to be a war protestor."

Neil rubbed his hands on his pristine shirt. "Is that what you thought?"

"Of course," Pamela said. "Every house he hit, we're all military families."

"Who happened to be flying flags, even at night." There was a bit of judgment in Neil's voice.

She knew what he was thinking. People who knew how to handle flags took them down at dusk. But she couldn't bear to touch hers. She hadn't asked Becky why hers remained up, but she would wager the reason was similar.

And it probably was for every other family Jeremy and his friends had targeted.

"That's the important factor?" she asked. "Night?"

"And beer," Neil said. "They lost a football game, went out and drank, and that fueled their anger. So they decided to act out."

"By burning flags?" Her voice rose.

"A few weeks before, they knocked down mailboxes. I'm going to hate to charge them. There won't be much left of the football team."

"That's all right," Pamela said bitterly. "Petty property crimes shouldn't take them off the roster long."

"It's going to be more than that," Neil said. "They're showing a destructive pattern. This one isn't going to be fun."

"For any of us," Pamela said.

***

HER HANDS WERE SHAKING as she left. She had wanted the crime to mean something. The flag had meant something to her. It should have meant something to them too.

God, Mom, for an old hippie, you're such a prude. Jenny's voice, so close that Pamela actually looked around, expecting to see her daughter's face.

"I'm not a prude," she whispered, and then realized she was reliving an old argument between them.

Sure you are. Judgmental and dried up. I thought you protested so that people could do what they wanted.

Pamela sat in the car, her creaky knees no longer holding her.

No, I protested so that people wouldn't have to die in another senseless war, she had said to her daughter on that May afternoon.

What year was that?

It had to be 1990, just before Jenny graduated from high school.

I'm not going to die in a stupid war, Jenny had said with such conviction that Pamela almost believed her. *We don't do wars any more. I'm going to get an education. That way, you don't have to struggle to pay for Travis. I know how hard it's been with Steve.*

Jenny, taking care of things. Jenny, who wasn't going to let her cash-strapped mother pay for her education. Jenny, being so sure of herself, so sure that the peace she'd known most of her life would continue.

To Jenny, going into the military to get a free education hadn't been a gamble at all.

Things'll change, honey, Pamela had said. *They always do.*

And by then I'll be out. I'll be educated, and moving on with my life.

Only Jenny hadn't moved on. She'd liked the military. After the First Gulf War, she'd gone to officer training, one of the first women to do it.

I'm a feminist, Mom, just like you, she'd said when she told Pamela.

Pamela had smiled, keeping her response to herself. She hadn't been that kind of feminist. She wouldn't have stayed in the military. She wasn't sure she believed in the military—not then.

And now? She wasn't sure what she believed. All she knew was that she had become a military mother, one who cried when a flag was burned.

Not just a flag.

Jenny's flag.

And that's when Pamela knew.

She wanted the crime to mean something, so she would make sure that it did.

***

SHE BROUGHT HER MEMORIES TO COURT. Not just the scrapbooks she'd kept for Jenny, like she had for all three kids, but the pictures from her own past, including the badly framed front page of the *Oregonian*.

Five burly boys had destroyed Jenny's flag. They stood in a row, their lawyers beside them, and pled to misdemeanors. Their parents sat on the blond bench seats in the 1970s courtroom. A reporter from the local paper took notes in the back. The judge listened to the pleadings.

Otherwise, the room was empty. No one cheered when the judge gave the boys six months of counseling. No one complained at the nine months of community service and even though a few of them winced when the judge announced the huge fines that they (and not their parents) had to pay, no one said a word.

Until Pamela asked if she could speak.

The judge—primed by Neil—let her.

Only she really didn't speak. She showed them Jenny. From the baby pictures to the dress uniform. From the brave eleven-year-old walking her brother to school to the dust-covered woman who had smiled with some Iraqi children in Baghdad.

Then Pamela showed them her *Oregonian* cover.

"I thought you were protesting," she said to the boys. "I thought you trying to let someone know that you don't approve of what your country is doing."

Her voice was shaking.

"I thought you were being patriotic." She shook her head. "And instead you were just being stupid."

To their credit, they watched her. They listened. She couldn't tell if they understood. If they knew how her heart ached—not that sharp pain she'd felt when she found the flag, but just an ache for everything she'd lost.

Including the idealism of the girl in the picture. And the idealism of the girl she'd raised.

When she finished, she sat down. And she didn't move as the judge gaveled the session closed. She didn't look up as some of the boys tried to apologize. And she didn't watch as their parents hustled them out of court.

Finally, Neil sat beside her. He picked up the framed *Oregonian* photograph in his big, scarred hands.

"Do you regret it?" he asked.

She touched the edge of the frame.

"No," she said.

"Because it was a protest?"

She shook her head. She couldn't articulate it. The anger, the rage, the fear she had felt then. Which had been nothing like the fear she had felt every day her daughter had been overseas.

The fear she felt now when she looked at Stephen's daughters and wondered what they'd chose in this never-ending war.

"If I hadn't burned that flag," she said, "I wouldn't have had Jenny."

Because she might have married Neil. And even if they had made babies, none of those babies would have been Jenny or Stephen or Travis. There would have been other babies who would have grown into other people.

Neil wasn't insulted. They had known each other too long for insults. Instead, he put his hand over hers. It felt warm and good and familiar. She put her head on his shoulder.

And they sat like that, until the court reconvened an hour later, for another crime, another upset family, and another broken heart.

The Moorhead House

*T*HE HOUSE ON THE HILL HAD CHRISTMAS LIGHTS. I stopped beside my van—white, with *DUSTY'S CLEANING* lettered in discreet gold. The van was camouflage—official enough, without advertising the kind of work I actually did—but people knew anyway. Hard to miss when the guy down the street offs himself, and a woman in a hazard suit, driving a van loaded with cleaning supplies, shows up a few days later.

But that day, I was alone. I was touring a cleaned scene, making sure my team had gotten every last bit. I wore my coveralls, a mask and three pairs of gloves, but I hadn't gone for the full treatment, thinking it unnecessary.

The neighborhood was solidly Oregon middle-class: old Victorians, 1930s bungalows, a few ranches; late-model cars, all probably bought on time; and lovely yards with only a little grass and lots of perennials. The kind of neighborhood a prospective buyer would look at and think of as a nice place to raise kids, the kind of place you grow old in, where your neighbors watch out for you, and keep track of every little thing.

But I'd been here four times in the ten years I'd owned this business—for the Hansen suicide (right in the living room, where the kids couldn't miss it. Bastard); the Palmer home-invasion-gone-wrong (the crime scene techs had missed the cat, curled up under the stove where it had apparently crawled to nurse its wounds); the well-known Bransted murder (the little girl had been dragged into a nearby garage and gutted there, mercifully after death); and the Moorhead ritual slaughter in the Victorian up the hill.

At least, the authorities believed it was a ritual slaughter. They never did find the bodies, although that place had four different high velocity spatters, and all sorts of ritualistic items—knives, black candles, destroyed crosses. That was the only case I'd ever been called to testify in, mostly because the members of that cult were convicted even though no one ever found the victims.

The murders had occurred over Christmas.

The first time I'd seen the Moorhead House, it'd been covered with Christmas lights like something out of a Hallmark greeting. All it needed had been two feet of snow, and a few carolers out front, holding their lanterns, their red-cheek faces upturned in wholesome rapturous praise.

My first partner'd quit after that job. Not that I blamed her. The Moorhead job had left me shaken too, and I'm not the shakable type. I'm a former firefighter and EMT, one of the first women in the state to do that kind of work, and I've battled both flame and discrimination with equal ferocity. I've seen what people can do to each other, and I've learned to accept it most of the time.

Since then, the Moorhead House had sold more than once, but no one had ever been able to live there long. So far as I knew, the place had been empty for years.

The Christmas lights bothered me.

They were up in the same place those original lights had been, white icicles—popular ten years ago—dripping down like melted frosting off the gables and the eaves of the Queen Anne.

So much like that dusky winter afternoon, when I'd seen the destruction for the first time.

Back then, I had no clue how to handle the destruction, the tears that cleaning a drop of blood from the back of a lamp might bring. I tried to pretend that I was just cleaning a place, a very filthy place, and I was beginning to realize that would never really function, that you couldn't stop the brain from wondering how it must've felt among the screams and the crashing and the glinting knife.

The state waited nearly a month before letting us in. By then, the place smelled like ancient rot and old blood.

That smell came back to me as I stared at those lights, promising a festive afternoon to anyone who would just march up the hill, and knock.

***

"WHO'S IN THE MOORHEAD HOUSE?" I asked when I got back to the office. "Office" is too big a word for the place: that makes it sound like we all have desks and secretaries and official nameplates. In reality, I have a tiny office and the rest of the place is two rooms—the front area with a desk, a phone, and a Coke machine that Debbie insisted on as well as a warehouse-style back room, filled with all manner of cleaning equipment, industrial strength showers, and five commercial washer and dryer sets.

Marcus sat behind the desk that afternoon. He's a big guy with a deep, reassuring voice, the kind folks like to hear when they've had a death in the family and decide to hire us themselves.

"Seen the lights, huh?" he said, leaning back in his chair and folding his massive hands over his surprisingly flat stomach.

"Yeah." I punched the Coke machine, and a root beer fell out.

We'd long ago bought the cola people out, filled the machine with our favorite cans, and shut off the payment mechanism. Now the thing works like an oversized (and expensive) refrigerator. I don't get rid of it though, because it's the only nifty part of our office.

"To be honest," I said, popping the top, "it scared me a little."

"Dwayne said that too."

I'd forgotten Dwayne worked the second part of that job—when the first set of new owners somehow got it into their heads that the tiny bones in the septic system belonged to the murdered family. The bones actually belonged to a family of squirrels. But by then, the crime scene techs had been back to the house and the lawn dug up. The mess was incredible, and the crime scene people decided to call us.

Not that it mattered to the first new owners. They sold as soon as the place was presentable again.

"How come that job weirded you out?" Marcus asked.

I shrugged, took a sip of the root beer, and said, "Sometimes I wonder why more jobs don't weird me out."

"Nice avoidance," he said. "Now answer."

I smiled at him. "Because there're no bodies."

"There're never any bodies when we go in," he said.

Which wasn't entirely true. There was that cat in the Palmer house and farther downtown, a stray dog left on the back porch. One of our other cleaning teams discovered an infant in a back closet, an infant which hadn't been part of the murder that the team had been cleaning up.

But I got Marcus's point. The bodies that we cleaned up after were long gone by the time we got to the house. We always knew what happened—we had to, so that we would know where to look for debris or spatter or pieces of skin—but we almost never saw the corpse.

"I think it would have been easier if there had been bodies." I set the root beer down. "It was the uncertainty."

Or maybe it had been my uncertainty. As an EMT, I'd pulled dying people out of car wrecks. As a firefighter, I'd been at houses where the children didn't get out, where the remaining person on the fifth floor refused to jump, where entire families died in their sleep.

But nothing prepared me for the emptiness of a crime scene. The moved furniture, the ruined rugs, the destroyed curtains. The toys that were pushed against the wall, the broken vases, the shattered lamps.

We couldn't repair that stuff. Our mission was to make sure no one could tell a violent or neglected death had happened in this place. And if the family still lived there, our mission was to make the place look like it had before what we euphemistically called, "The Event."

But the Moorhead House was the first place I worked without a family to move back into it or without an owner overseeing the job we did on the rental property.

No family left, no extended family leaving messages on my machine, no potential owners waiting to rebuild the place according to their new vision.

I tried not to look at the Moorhead House as I drove to my next job. It wasn't far away—another suicide, damn the holiday season—and from the back door of a kitchen that hadn't been cleaned since 1978, I could see the lights of the Moorhead House against the rain-darkened sky.

I tried to ignore it, to concentrate on the life lost, the loneliness that seemed to be the cause. This man hadn't been found for nearly two weeks, which put his death on Thanksgiving Day. The remains of a small turkey and the store-bought pumpkin pie confirmed that.

He had family—an estranged wife who hadn't seen him in nearly thirty years, two children now grown, and parents who sounded genuinely hurt when they hired us over the phone.

I'd learned, though, that genuine hurt sometimes sounded brusque or businesslike, not thick with tears. And I wondered about a man whose house was so dirty that the neighbors didn't complain about the odor because they were used to odors coming from the place.

I never told my co-workers that I thought about the dead as if I were the last person who would remember them. Sometimes, perhaps, I was. Certainly the family of that man wouldn't know how bleak his life was at the end. Even if one of us told them, they wouldn't be able to imagine the piled up papers, the half-written letters, the battered but comfortable chair in front of the TV.

I recognized this house because it was a filthy version of my own.

My place is spotless. Because my hours are long and my moods uncertain, I don't keep a pet. I have the battered but comfortable single chair in front of a too-big television, only it's in my basement, not the center of the living room.

If someone asked me, I'd never admit to being lonely. Usually I don't mind.

Except on difficult days, days when I'm cleaning out someone else's solitary home.

***

THE INVITATION CAME TWO DAYS LATER. The city's annual bash, held for the contractors and private firms that kept the city running, was always a big deal. The planners spared no expense. Once they rented a yacht to follow the old ferry route across the river. Another time, they commandeered the largest, trendiest nightclub in the city. And one time—the only time (because too many people complained)—they held a beautiful secular service at the city's historic Presbyterian Church.

This year, however. This year's site was a stunner.

Debbie handed me the invite not three minutes after the mail arrived. I was sitting in my office, enjoying a rare moment of quiet. I had that week's checks spread in front of me. I was thinking about the bank deposit, and having a healthy bank balance at the Christmas holidays for the first time since I'd opened the business.

"Boss," Debbie said.

I looked up. Her normally dusky skin had paled to an abnormal gray color. She held the invitation between her thumb and forefinger as if it smelled bad.

It didn't look bad. In fact, I recognized it. We usually didn't get formal invitations here, not the kind with the gold foil borders and the hand calligraphy.

"What's wrong?" I asked.

She handed me the invite. It was on a stiff cardboard stock that felt like expensive parchment. I glanced at the language, familiar with it after ten years of parties.

"The annual party," I said. "So?"

"Look where they're holding it."

I did. And felt the blood leave my face as well.

The Moorhead House.

"Get me the envelope," I said.

She went back to reception. I could see her through my door, rummaging through the wastebasket. When she finally found the envelope, she carried it back to me in the same way she had carried the invite itself—thumb and forefinger, as if the entire thing would infect her.

I took the envelope from her. It was made of a matching stock and had a metered city hall postmark from the day before. If someone had sent this as a joke, they would have had to duplicate the card stock and use the city hall postage meter, which gets guarded like crazy so that city hall employees don't use it for personal letters.

"Crap," I said, and reached for the phone.

I dialed the RSVP number at the bottom of the invite. After a few rings, I got the voice mail of a person I didn't know. I hung up, and dialed the deputy mayor, Greg Raabe. We had gone to college together. We'd even dated a few times before I had found my calling and before he had met his wife.

His secretary picked up immediately, and when she heard it was me, put me through even faster.

"Greg," I said without preamble, "what's this about the Christmas party at the Moorhead House? Do you remember what happened there?"

"I remember," he said, which was not the response I expected. I expected some political dance or an actual lapse of memory. The fact that he answered—and sounded disgusted—meant that he had fielded more than one call about this.

"Don't you think this is a little inappropriate?"

"What I think doesn't matter," he said. "It's a done deal."

"Why?" I asked.

"Because," he said, "the city bought the building. They plan to turn it into a museum."

***

THAT WAS THE THING about the Moorhead House, the thing no one talked about any more. Shortly after the family died, the National Register of Historic Places placed the house on its registry. Apparently someone had gone through the entire historic preservation rigmarole in the years before the murders.

Fortunately for me, the certification came after we cleaned the place up. If it had come before, the job would have taken much longer, and the city would have been billed for a great deal more money.

Historic preservation crime scene cleaning required an entirely different use of chemicals, several kinds of oversight, and all sorts of paperwork, things I'd just managed to avoid.

I'd managed to overlook most of that and had, in fact, forgotten it, until Greg Raabe had said the word "museum."

The Moorhead House had been the first home built on this side of the river. The fabulously wealthy Moorheads had made their money in various enterprises in the Oregon territory, from logging to mining to trading supplies. Then they bought up the land surrounding the river, and sold it, piecemeal, to settlers coming down the Oregon Trail.

The Moorheads kept large portions of the land, however, much of it near the river, so that they could control the ferries (the only way to get across and head to Portland, even then the state's major city). The river also gave them added control of the logging industry. In those days, logs floated down the river to be collected at sloughs which were also owned by the Moorheads. Over time, the river land became a center for what little industry the city had, and the rents made the Moorheads even wealthier.

But they became enchanted with their wealth, and wanted a lot more power than owning a single small city would give them. The great-grandsons of the original family moved to Portland, where they bought even grander houses on even grander hills. Their sons became politicians, and their children became drug-addicted deadbeats who had every privilege.

Somewhere along the way, the holdings here got sold. Then the houses in Portland went, and finally, the famous family, now down to an infamous few, had only enough left to maintain their townhouses in Washington D.C.

The Moorhead House, symbol of the wealth and power of a bygone age, had—even before the federal government decided to protect it—become the symbol of death and destruction in the modern age.

"A museum?" I asked.

"People love a mystery," Greg said in that dryly bland voice, the one I always thought of as his political voice. "And the house is truly historical. The museum will have one room dedicated to the murders, but it'll be up-stairs. The rest'll talk about city history, the impact of the Moorheads, and the way that this part of Oregon once seemed like the center of the universe."

Then I knew he was being sarcastic. He never used that phrase in serious conversation.

"Whose idea was this?" I asked.

"You read about it in the papers?" he asked as if that was an answer.

"No," I said.

"Then think about it."

I did, and it only took me a minute to understand. The mayor had done this. The mayor, Louise Vogel, had set herself up as a minor dictator, much to the disgust of everyone outside of her party and even some within.

She had the benefit of being one of the few people in the city who would take the job, which paid next to nothing for the amount of work it took. Greg had be-come deputy mayor as a sort of oversight position, but she had defanged him quickly. She owned much of the council, bought, I was told, with a combination of blood money and blackmail threats. The woman knew how to run small city politics.

"Why in the world would Louise want the Moorhead House as a museum?" I asked.

"I have no idea," Greg said. "Makes as much sense to me as holding a Christmas party there. So, are you coming?"

"I cleaned the place, Greg," I said softly. "I had to tes-tify at the trial."

"Oh." He was silent for a moment. Then he sighed. "I'm supposed to jolly people into attending."

"Has it been working?"

"So far," he said. "Apparently, people like to pretend they're not interested in death houses, but they really are."

Unless they see the houses in full aftermath.

"I suppose it'll be a grand affair," I said, mimicking his dry voice.

"It'll be memorable, that's for sure," he said, and signed off.

I held onto the phone for a moment longer, mostly to fend off Debbie's questions. As she listened to my conversation, she seemed to have gotten ahold of herself. She shook her head and shifted from foot to foot, as if she could barely contain herself.

I set the receiver down. "It's no joke."

She swallowed. "Are we going?"

The city's party was always the highlight of our year.

"Greg says the party'll be memorable," I said.

"People will talk about it for a long time," she said.

I adjusted some of the checks in front of me. My pleasure in my unusual wealth at year's end had faded.

"Let's make attendance optional this year," I said. "And before anyone agrees to go, make sure they know that the party'll be at Moorhead House."

"Okay." Debbie started to leave my office, then she paused at the door. "You going?"

"I don't know," I said, and realized, to my surprise, that I had just spoken the truth.

***

I suppose, politically, I should have said I was going to go. My job, after all, was to make buildings habitable again. Part of habitable was holding festive events—weddings, bar mitzvahs, Christmas parties.

But habitable was different than comfortable. And habitable wasn't always possible.

Places like Moorhead House were notorious, and notoriety lingered long after the physical examples of the crimes had disappeared.

In the end, it was my curiosity that took me there. I wanted to see the house in all its glory. I wanted to know if it could still have glory.

And I wanted to know exactly what Louise Vogel was up to this time.

***

No one else from the office wanted to go. Debbie actually called me ghoulish, even though I wasn't the person holding the party. Dwayne looked at me with pity, asked me if I was sure, and when I said I was, he visibly shuddered. Then he told me, quietly, that he'd never go in that house again, not even if I paid him to do so.

In the end, Marcus went with me, mostly because he was curious. He'd been hired long after I did the first part of the Moorhead House job, but he was there for the tail end of the trial, and for Dwayne's run at the tiny bones in the sewers. Marcus told me he'd always wanted to go inside, and acknowledged that it was an unhealthy curiosity, based as much on the missing bodies as it was on the effect the entire place had had on our office.

He picked me up at eight. I'd forgotten how well he cleaned up. He wore a long jacket over dress pants—a modern suit that harked back to the Old West—and instead of looking like a football player stuffed into his younger brother's clothing, he looked like something out of *GQ*.

I felt dowdy in comparison. I wore a black velvet dress, and I decked it with a red scarf and some glittery (but fake) jewelry I'd inherited from my great aunt. My matching black velvet heels required, of all things, dusting, and I had to run out an hour before the party to buy panty hose without runs or pulls.

Marcus waited inside my foyer while I dithered over coats and purses, feeling more like a girl-girl than I had for awhile. Once upon a time, I had cared about things like make-up and matching purses with shoes, but I had lost that at nineteen, when I'd come home from college to find my mother dead of a stroke on the kitchen floor.

She had been there for a week. My parents were divorced—my father lived in another state—and I was an only child. I had come home to surprise my mother, and instead, she had surprised me.

Marcus had a 1960s Mustang that he took out for special occasions, and apparently this ranked as one of those. He drove to the Moorhead House in silence. Normally, we would have chattered the entire way—Marcus and I share the same taste in movies, books, and politics—but those subjects paled in comparison to the house.

The Mustang rode lower than my van, so the view of the Moorhead House as we turned onto the street below seemed even more impressive that usual. This close to Christmas, you'd think other homes on the block would have decorations on the windows or lights strung outside, but the Moorhead House seemed to be the only one with Christmas spirit.

I looked up at the place as we started toward the drive, and those icicle lights still sent a chill through me. I almost told Marcus to turn around and I'd buy him dinner at a nearby steakhouse so we wouldn't waste the dress-up clothes, but I didn't. I knew better than to seem weak in front of one of my employees.

I'd learned that lesson as a female fire-fighter. Even when you felt uncomfortable, you took a deep breath and went into the smoke. To do anything less meant you couldn't perform your duties.

And somehow, this party had become one of my duties.

***

WE WERE ARRIVING DELIBERATELY LATE. I hated showing up early to any party. Marcus pulled the Mustang into the circular drive, and my breath caught.

Some things were different: the hedges had been clipped to the bone and did not have lights hanging from them as they had that murderous Christmas season. Signs had been planted in what had been the yard but was now obviously going to be a garden, warning guests to stay on the paths. The signs had been hand-calligraphed, and looked expensive. They even had little drawings of holly around the edges.

I hated them.

Marcus looked at me as he got out of the Mustang, and then he grinned like a little boy who was about to do something wrong.

"Ready, boss?" he asked.

I'd never be ready, but I smiled gamely and put my hand on his massive arm. He helped me pick my way across the path. The air was cold and damp, but the pine boughs near the house gave off a Christmasy scent that I hadn't expected.

Suddenly I felt younger than I had in years, almost like that girl I'd left in my mother's kitchen, and my heart lifted. A party was just what I needed. If I could forget the house, or at least look on its new role as host as a personal victory, I might be able to have a good time.

We stepped onto the porch together. Inside the frosted glass windows, we could see shapes moving against yellow light.

My stomach clenched, and I swallowed convulsively.

I wasn't sure I could do this.

Marcus gave me a sideways glance. "You okay?"

I nodded because I couldn't answer. He knocked on the door.

Someone pulled it open and the smells of burning wood and baking cookies filled the air. Laughter came along with Mel Torme's voice, singing about Jack Frost nipping at noses. The man who opened the door had a Santa hat over graying hair. The hat didn't go with his exquisitely tailored suit.

He held a glass clearly filled with eggnog in one hand. With the other, he gestured toward the interior. "Merry, merry!"

"Happy, happy," Marcus said, making fun of him.

But the man didn't seem to notice. He clapped Marcus on the back as we walked inside.

The place was transformed. If I hadn't known it was the house in which I'd spent a week cleaning, I wouldn't have recognized it. To my right, the curved staircase was once again the center of the house. Someone had wrapped garlands of holly around the mahogany banister, probably with no thought to how old, how rare or how valuable the wood was.

People stood on the stairs, holding drinks, talking, some looking at the portraits hung over the stairs, others heading up to see what else the house had in store.

Coats were piled on top of the telephone seat built against the wall. The carpets were gone, revealing wood floors that matched the wood trim throughout the house.

I couldn't imagine what it had cost to clean the floors. I had cleaned the carpets and recommended their removal, but no one had done that—at least not for the first family which bought the place. I had warned the realtors that if anyone took up the carpets, they might find horrible stains beneath. I had removed the rugs myself in the upstairs bedroom where two of the family members had bled to death (there was no saving those rugs, and no attempt to), but the ones down here had had bloody footprints and drag marks, and other stains that I never could quite identify.

"You're staring," Marcus whispered.

At least, I thought he whispered it, although he might have spoken in a normal tone. The party noises going on around us made it hard to hear much more than the rumble of conversation. The music was classy and so were the people around me. Hard to believe most of them spent their days in jeans and overalls or uniforms paid for by the city.

"Sorry," I whispered.

"Is it different?" he asked.

"Yeah."

I led Marcus into what had once been the front parlor. The pocket doors were gone, along with most of the walls that contained them, so now the front and back parlors were one room (with an arch) that modern people would call the living room.

The furniture was fake period with a fainting couch, a regular couch, and overstuffed armchairs. Too many tables crowded the bay window, and on those tables stood food of all sorts from cookies and sliced pies to small unidentifiable appetizers and toothpicked bits of fruit and cheese.

Marcus grabbed a small plate, shaking it with surprise. "China."

"Nothing but the best," I muttered, and doubted he could hear me.

I couldn't eat, even if I wanted to. I left him there, debating whether to have strawberries dipped in chocolate or chocolate-covered cherry truffles. From a passing waiter carrying a tray of beverages on his outstretched palm, I snatched a flute of champagne, carrying it with me as I went from room to room.

The place had clearly been professionally decorated. From the furniture to the draped pine boughs and hanging mistletoe, the interior looked like something out of *House Beautiful*.

The Christmas tree, at the far wall of what had been the back parlor, took up so much space that it seemed to be growing out of the floor. It was decorated in silver bows, tinsel, and little silver lights that blinked on and off. An embarrassing display of packages hid the lower branches.

I knew from previous parties that the packages would be gone by the night's end, a mound of paper left for someone else to clean up, and the gifts would seem less impressive unwrapped than they did at this moment.

A *Do-Not-Enter* sign had been taped to the swinging kitchen door, the only infelicity in the entire place. I ignored it, and went inside anyway, drawn by the smells of baking cookies. Small women in rented tuxedos and looking hot, wiped hair away from their faces. Two coaxed a stainless steel dishwasher to take more dishes. Another woman bent over the stove, and yet another was placing crudités on a silver tray.

Men, as tall as the women were small, picked up the trays. The men also wore tuxes, but on them, the tuxes looked natural. Maybe because they were in traditional serving roles, where the women, stuck in the kitchen, should have been in simple black dresses with aprons to complete the servant illusion.

"You're not supposed to be here," said the woman filling the trays.

"That's all right," I said. "I used to work here."

One of the men looked at me sharply. He frowned a little, as if wondering how anyone could have worked here, given the history of the house. Or maybe I was reading too much into a slight reaction. Maybe he thought my lame excuse for being in the kitchen was just that. I smiled at him, and slipped out of the way.

The kitchen was dramatically different, remodeled about the time of the bones discovered in the sewer drain. The stove was restaurant quality, the refrigerator one of those stainless steel subzero monstrosities that looked like it could eat an entire room.

Everything was different, and somehow I found that more disconcerting than the Christmas decorations around front. When I had cleaned this place, the kitchen had been my haven—the only room without much blood in the entire house, and that blood only came from the detectives and crime scene techs. Harmless, innocuous drops, left by people who were trying to solve the crime, not the people who had created it.

My stomach was churning. The smell of food was making me ill. I pushed open the swinging door and stepped back into the living room.

Marcus was talking to a pretty woman in a slinky blue dress. Louise was standing near the tree, gesturing at the presents. She looked even thinner than usual, her face bony, her black hair pulled into a tight bun.

Her gaze caught mine, flat and challenging. I lifted my still full glass in a silent toast. She smiled—a real and warm smile, something I had never seen from her before—and raised her glass as well. We drank in concert from separate parts of the room as if we were old friends.

"I see you've kissed and made up." Greg Raabe, the deputy mayor who had told me about this debacle, had sidled up beside me. He knew how much I disliked Louise, and how that feeling seemed to be mutual.

I turned to him and smiled. He no longer looked like the boy I'd dated in school. That boy had been reedy slender and blond, with no muscles at all. His bright blue eyes had dominated his face.

The eyes remained the same, dominating and filled with personality, but the rest of him had changed. He was as heavy as he had once been slight, and in place of those visible ribs were rock-hard abs from all the weights he lifted. He ate to compensate for the tension, I think, because he didn't drink or smoke, and to compensate for the eating, he exercised.

"There was no kissing," I said to him, happier than I wanted to be to see him. "I just saluted her, that's all. This is quite the party."

"This is quite the expense," he said. "Imagine what the council will say when they see this on the city budget."

I grinned. "Fortunately, that's not my job."

"But it could be mine," he said, looking at her talking to the man near the presents. "I was kind of hoping that once she had her stepping stone to the governorship, I could become mayor."

"One party won't get in the way," I said.

"You're assuming that this party is the only budget item that'll bother them." He sighed and grabbed his own champagne flute from a passing waiter.

I looked up at the waiter as he went by. It was the man who had frowned in the kitchen. He looked familiar. His skin was a ruddy color that wasn't common in the Pacific Northwest, except among people who worked on the ocean. He had a square jaw, and hard cheekbones, the kind I always associated with those 1930s pictures of Aryan youth.

"Know him?" Greg asked.

"He looks familiar," I said as he went into the kitchen. "Does he to you?"

"In a generic waiterly way." Greg smiled. "I told Louise we should have dancing, but she didn't listen to me."

"There's no room," I said. Besides, Greg wouldn't have been able to dance with me even if there had been music. His wife Emma pretended that the fact we dated didn't bother her, when, in fact, it was very clear that it did.

I scanned the room, but didn't see her. "Is Emma upstairs?"

The smile left his face. "She wouldn't come."

"Because of the house?" I asked.

"Because of the separation." His voice was low. "She doesn't like my ambitions."

Emma had always wanted Greg to settle down and make money. He had always been more interested in public service than in making monetary use of his expensive law degree. Apparently the fights had come to a head.

"When did you separate?" I asked.

He shushed me and whispered. "Not everyone knows."

"Sorry," I said.

"It happened last week. I have an apartment near city hall, which I'd had anyway. I guess I knew this was coming."

Everyone had known this was coming, maybe even from the moment the vows were taken. But Greg seemed quietly devastated.

I put my hand on his shoulder, startled to feel the same kind of muscles I had felt on Marcus. "I'm really sorry," I said again.

Greg grinned. The look didn't quite meet his eyes. "No, you're not. You never liked Emma."

Not many of his friends had, and I always figured the ones who had liked her just pretended for Greg's sake.

"I am sorry," I said. "For you. This is hard."

"Yeah," he said, and then sighed. "Duty beckons."

Duty didn't, but Louise did. She was waving him over with a hand so manicured I could see the shine of the nail polish from here. Time for the packages. I hoped they got to my name quickly. I was ready to leave.

Marcus had left his new conquest and came over beside me. "Did you check the upstairs?"

I shook my head. I hadn't forgotten the upstairs, but I didn't see the need to torture myself. "I ducked into the kitchen for a while."

Which reminded me of the waiter, whom I no longer saw. "Did you notice that waiter, the one who looked like he'd been a member of the Hitler Youth?"

"No," Marcus said. "Why?"

Greg had clapped his hands for quiet. I sighed. I knew this drill. First they'd demand silence, then they'd hand out gifts. Louise worked off a list. I had noted last year that the city contractors like me got one of two things: an espresso maker (if the city had spent a lot of money on you) or a care basket filled with all kinds of city products, like salmon and some of our famous cheese and locally grown filberts.

I, of course, had gotten a care basket, even though the city spent a lot of money on our services. I thought that it was merely an oversight, then Greg had reminded me that we weren't listed in the budget. We were buried in other line items. So no one really knew how much money we made cleaning up local property except maybe Debbie and me.

Greg started calling out names. The man beside Louise handed out the packages, and Louise kept charge of the list. People walked up, got large gaudily wrapped gifts, and then walked away, grinning.

Marcus rolled his eyes. "How long is this going to take?"

"Usually about an hour," I said. "You want to go back and make goo-goo eyes at that sweet young thing?"

"She's hard to talk to," he said.

"Because?" I asked.

His face shut down. "Because I told her what I do."

That was one of the major drawbacks to our business. People thought we were on the level of grave diggers and morticians. Even the popularity of programs like *CSI*, which made one small aspect of death work glamorous, didn't spill over to us.

"Tough break," I said.

He shrugged. "Anyone with reactions like that's too shallow for me."

But he didn't sound sincere. And then he took my champagne and finished it for me. I watched him drink another, and decided that at some point in the evening, I'd have to wrestle the Mustang's keys from him, and get us home.

***

IT TOOK TWO MORE HOURS before we could leave. I never did see the waiter again, but I got absorbed in my present—a small wireless weather forecasting kit, with barometer and thermometer, something that actually appealed to my scientific sensibilities. Marcus slowed on the drinks—he'd found another pretty woman to chat up, and apparently this time, he didn't make the mistake of telling her what he did—and I didn't want to interrupt his rhythm.

I looked at the stairs twice, but I didn't go up them. I searched for Greg, and found Louise instead. She was leaning against a side of the arch, holding but not drinking a glass of champagne. She watched the proceeding with tired eyes.

When she saw me, she smiled again.

I wasn't sure I liked that. Two real smiles from Louise in one evening. Something had to be wrong.

"It's going well, isn't it?" she asked.

"Better than I would have thought," I said.

She sipped the champagne—or pretended to. Maybe that was one of her secrets. Pretending to drink when everyone around her got blotto.

"It's a tribute to you people," she said.

At first, I thought she meant the little people, the non-politicos, and then I realized she actually meant us, Dusty's Cleaning.

"Thanks," I said, glancing at those stairs.

"I mean it," she said. "This place is cheerful. Who would have thought?"

I looked at her. Her entire face looked tired, and she was too thin. Maybe it was the strain of the party, or maybe something else had gone wrong in her life. I wasn't sure, and I wasn't about to ask.

"It's what we do," I said.

"Exorcise the ghosts," she said, as if in agreement.

But the ghosts weren't exorcised for me. They still lurked beneath the party favors and the seasonal joy.

When this crowd left, and the caterers finished, when the last staff member shut off the lights, the house would revert to its post-murder self. The high-velocity spatter would paint itself on the walls, the cries would echo in the upstairs bedroom, and the blood would seep into the rugs.

I shuddered. I couldn't help it.

Of course, Louise noticed. "Does it still bother you?"

"Sometimes," I said before I could stop myself, "I think places like this should be burned."

Louise frowned at me. "That's an odd sentiment, coming from you."

I shrugged. "There are some places," I said, "that never get entirely clean."

***

THE DREAM CAME AS IT OFTEN DID. It started with my mother. She was on the floor of our kitchen, the smell of Lemon Pledge filling the air. When she saw me, she stood, apologized, and offered to cook. I thought it inappropriate to have the newly dead make the meal, and I told her so, even though I knew I was disappointing her.

She slipped out the side door, and as she did, she said, "You'll never see me again."

Only as I mulled the words, I realized she hadn't said "see," she had said "find." *You'll never find me again.*

Then, in the transitionless magic of dreams, I stood in the foyer of the Moorhead House. The place smelled of weeks-old blood and voided bowels. Beneath those smells was that of rotted flesh.

As I stood there, I existed on two levels: the woman standing in the foyer, and the woman who knew every inch of that house, the one who had cleaned it all and who would, if she wasn't careful, become obsessed with it.

The walls in the upstairs bedroom had a spatter pattern that looked like a post-modernist painting. I knew that it was spray—a knife or something sharp pierced an artery, and the blood sprayed before the dying man? woman? child? turned so that the rest of the blood would shoot against a different wall.

Then the dream changed. The waiter stared at me with those cold blue eyes. I'd seen them before. Not at a party where he was curiously out of place but at the trial.

He sat in the second row from the back, and watched my every move. His face wasn't ruddy then, but he was thinner, sadder, and his eyes had fear in them.

I couldn't look at him as I testified. He made me nervous.

That day, everyone made me nervous.

I thought nothing of it.

You'll never find me again.

Then the scene changed once more. My mother's kitchen, without her body lying on the middle of the floor, looked like a happy place—painted yellow, spotlessly clean. Only a chair had moved, tilted away from the table, as if its occupant left suddenly.

Add the body to the picture, sprawled along the tile, arms thrown backward, fluids staining the clothes, and the moved chair was ominous. Had she stood because she felt ill? Or had she simply been crossing to the refrigerator when her body gave out?

Or had she been laying there, helpless, only able to slide a chair a little toward her, thinking maybe it would help her up, but the experiment didn't work, and she remained—alone—on her back, until she breathed her last.

I sat up, not sure exactly when I woke, when the dream ended and the thinking began.

We could guess about the bodies in the Moorhead House, but we didn't know. We didn't know if the ritual items—the desecrated religious symbols, the black candles, the knives—had been added later to throw us off. Because they had been removed as evidence before I arrived, I didn't even know if they'd been covered with spatter, proving they'd been in position before the family died.

I did know that they left no impression wherever they'd been. There were no knife-sized holes in the spatter pattern, no black candle wax on the side tables.

Only the blood and the stink and the sense that something horrible had happened here.

I turned on my too-large television. One of the get-rich-quick real estate gurus hawked his no-money down method. As house after house flashed on the screen, I wondered what secrets those houses held.

Over time, the secrets faded.

All bodies disappeared, forgotten, lost.

Did the people who owned my mother's house now enjoy their kitchen? Did they walk easily over the spot where she had spent her last hours? Did they wonder how long her body had been there, waiting for someone to find her?

More importantly, did they care?

And that's when my stomach turned, when the crazy food that I had eaten backed up into my throat.

No one had cared at the Moorhead House party. If the murders were mentioned, it was with a salacious edge, as if the deaths were part of a setting, added for the party-goers' enjoyment.

Five people were missing, presumed dead—presumed because no one lost that much blood and lived.

But the police hadn't tested every drop. Only a few to make DNA comparisons, enough to build a case without a body—one of the toughest murder cases to bring. The cult, arrested, charged, and pulled off the street for life, had continually maintained their innocence.

I hadn't been able to look at them either when I testified—malnourished, scared twenty-somethings who'd used too many drugs and lived too close to the crime scene.

People had seen them in the house, but no one had seen them on the night of the murders.

No one had seen anything that night, even though the house dominated that hillside.

Even though the house dominated the entire town.

***

THE NEXT MORNING, we had a fire-clean. Mostly smoke and water damage. The apartment, on the lower floor of a large complex, had lost its kitchen, and the rest was ruined. But the upper floors were still livable if we could get the stench out, which we could.

The apartments had been evacuated, but they still held the stuff of people's lives—dolls scattered on a bedroom floor, slippers kicked aside in someone's haste to escape, a half-eaten pizza on a scarred coffee table.

I surveyed the damage, realized the cleaning would be one of our easier jobs, and called in a junior team. Then I went back to the office, and pulled the Moorhead files.

The image of my mother's kitchen chair, fresh from my dream, haunted me. We had approached the Moorhead scene with a single assumption: that the family had been slaughtered there in a ritualistic way, and the bodies had then been moved.

But what if there had been no ritual? What if this had been a crime of passion? Blood was everywhere in that house, except the kitchen, an oddity explained at the time by the ritualistic nature of the deaths.

I didn't have crime scene photos, but I did have my photos of the scene. It was the early days of my business; I did before-and-after photos for prospective clients.

The before photos were vicious and dark, grimmer than I remembered. But the blood spatter, the filth left from violent death, was much as my memory held it—a long, continuous spray, followed by real spatter, arcing as the blood pulsed from someone's body.

In one photo, my hand pressed on the rug, releasing the blood contained within. In another, the rivulets of blood went down the stairs, drops alongside heading away from the scene.

What had the police tested? What had they ignored?

I thumbed through until I found the bathrooms. They, like the bedrooms, were thick with blood. The toilet, the bathtub, and the sinks had light spray, but nothing inside the porcelain basins, suggesting that no one had cleaned up there.

No one had cleaned in the kitchen either.

I stared at the images, trying to recall the lesson of the dream. Take away my expectations, and what did I see?

A charnel house.

A place where blood was allowed to flow freely and for some time.

I closed the file and leaned on it, my stomach as queasy as it had been the night before. I rubbed my eyes, sighed heavily, and picked up the phone.

**

I HAD A LOT OF CONTACTS at the police department. Early on, they had considered me part of the brotherhood, mostly because of my EMT and fire training, and they handed out my cards to grieving widows and distraught adult children.

Over time, several officers would call me before the city did, letting me know I had a job on the way, and preparing me, so that I could put the proper team on it. If the case was sensitive, I often did the work myself. That way, if I found overlooked or lost evidence, I knew that it would be handled correctly. Mostly, I would leave it alone, and place a call on my cell. The forensic teams would arrive quickly because, I'd learned, it was me. My assistants often didn't get the same kind of respect.

Still, asking to see files in a case that had been closed for years was a sensitive thing. It irked all of us involved that we hadn't found the bodies, but, we had consoled ourselves, we had found the killers. I had taken this case as personally as the detectives who had worked it, and we all confessed late one night in the local cop bar that this was the case that haunted us.

Detective Jeffrey Foreno was the only one who had ever expressed doubts about the case. He had openly questioned whether the cult had done the killings. After all, he said, no blood was found in their hidey hole. No knives, no black candles. And nothing suggested they had been on the property that night. It had all been supposition and circumstance, fear and small-town politics.

He had been shushed pretty quickly.

So he was the one I went to that morning.

He was approaching retirement. The lines in his face were deep and grooved, accented by the white stubble he'd forgotten to shave off before coming to work. The rest of his hair was black and thick, in need of a cut. His eyes, once sharp and alert, were blood-shot, and when he saw me, he sighed.

"I knew someone would want to resurrect the dead."
He leaned back in his chair, his hands folded over his
stomach. "Just didn't expect it to be you."

I'd told him once I dreamed about cleaning the
house, about the way the blood came back, as if the
walls never wanted to give it up. He'd told me that he
dreamed of the case too—of the Christmas tree that
hadn't existed even though the outside of the house
had been exquisitely decorated, of the lack of food in
the kitchen, of the empty pet bowls, cleaned and stored
in a dusty pantry.

"Why did you think someone would bring up the
case?" I asked, sitting across from him.

He gave me one of those sideways looks that always
made me nervous. Even with blood-shot eyes, Jeffrey
Foreno had a way of looking all the way to your soul.

"The party," I said.

He pointed at me which, in Jeff language meant *You
got it in one.*

"How come you didn't go?" I asked.

"It felt like dancing on someone's grave." Then he
gave me that look again and his lips thinned. "You went."

I nodded. "Figured I had to. It had been my job to
make sure no one noticed what had happened there."

He didn't move nor did his expression change. "Did
it work?"

I shrugged. "I think Louise was using the murders to
give the place ambience."

"The power of rubbernecking," he said.

"Yeah." I wouldn't have put it so crassly, but he was right. Maybe that was why I hadn't gone upstairs, why I refused to look at the rooms where the police had assumed most of the killings had taken place. Downstairs, the tree, the presents, the food, masked the prurience that went into the planning. Upstairs, the unvarnished truth—the naked interest on the hands of people more fortunate than the dwellers of the Moorhead House— would have been readily apparent.

"Did it open old wounds?" he asked.

I shook my head quickly, not sure I wanted to examine my answer to that question too closely.

"So you just came today out of curiosity," he said as if he didn't believe it.

"I came because I saw someone." I told him about the waiter, the way the man had looked at me, both at the party and at the courthouse.

Foreno shrugged. "Maybe he was one of the rubberneckers. Some people make certain murder cases into their hobby."

"I know," I said. "But sometimes there's more to it."

He frowned at me.

"Remember anyone involved in the case who looked like that?"

"Like a perfect World War II German? Can't say as I do."

Put that way, I wouldn't have recognized him either. "I'd like to look through the file."

"Be my guest," Fareno said. "It's not going to bother anyone. Unless you find something."

136

We grinned at each other. Then he led me to records, got me the closed case files, and signed off so that I could work.

***

THE MOORHEAD FILE TOOK UP FIVE BOXES, most of them police and evidence reports. I gave the evidence reports a cursory glance, and saw exactly what I suspected: the assumptions began with the murder of the family and went from there. Most of the blood evidence was scraped from the wall of the bedroom—the crime scene tech's reasoning was simple: he didn't want to deal with the inevitable carpet fibers in the blood pool. Although, to his credit, he did cut carpet swatches as well, and stored them in one of the refrigeration units at the crime lab. Unless someone needed the space, the evidence might still be there.

I searched through the boxes until I found what I was looking for. Pictures. Not of the house, but of the family.

Five members—husband, wife, three children, the oldest being fifteen, the youngest twelve. Speculation by the investigating officer was that one or all of the children had had contact with the cult.

I stared at the father. His face was bony and Aryan too, almost but not quite the same as the waiter I had seen. The eldest son, fourteen, looked like his father or might have if he lived. That heavy bone structure was unusual, at least in these parts. I thumbed through the documents to see if there were other family members in the vicinity.

No one had located any. Pages and pages of police interviews, with neighbors, co-workers, friends, did not include anyone from the family.

Then I looked at the mug shots of the cult members. I remembered those faces from the trial as well. Young, confused, ravaged, they made me wonder whether those kids were vulnerable because they were following the wrong leader or whether they had followed the wrong leader because they were vulnerable.

I closed the boxes, feeling more uncertain than I had before I started. I put them back, and went upstairs to say good-bye to Foreno.

"Find anything?" he asked.

I shook my head.

"Let it rest." Then he gave me that look. "You're not going to, are you?"

"Who inherited the house?" I asked.

"No one," he said. "The state ended up with it."

"No family," I said.

"None that we could find." He tapped a pen against the top of his desk. "And before you ask, let me tell you I remember this because it seemed so damn odd. Two middle-aged parents with no family at all. No one remembered any grandparents or aunts and uncles visiting the kids. These people were an island."

"Their money went to the state too?"

"Eventually," he said. "Not that there was much of it."

"In a house like that?"

"Mortgaged and credit cards. The furniture wasn't even worth anything. The appearance of money, but no real money."

"Don't you find that strange?"

"Always have," he said.

"The guy I saw," I said, "looks a lot like the father."

Foreno cursed, then leaned back in his chair. "You sure?"

"It's not him," I said. "There're differences."

"Family differences?"

"I'd've thought they were brothers or cousins," I said.

Foreno frowned. Then he reached to the left and opened his bottom desk drawer. From my vantage, standing, I could see a dozen accordion files, all filled with manila folders. He thumbed through the files, then pulled out one folder.

He slid it to me, and stood.

"You want some lunch?" he asked. "I'm buying."

I looked at him with surprise.

He nodded toward a chair in the corner. "It'll take you a while to go through that."

"A sandwich would be nice," I said.

He grabbed his suit coat, then headed out the door. As he left, he pulled the door closed, so that someone passing by wouldn't be able to see me.

I found that curious, but not as curious as the file. It was thick with newspaper clippings and computer print-outs, some more than a decade old.

Cult killings, ritual murders, and bodiless cases. This was Foreno's comparison file. He was right: it took me quite a bit of time to read it. He managed to return with the sandwiches and we ate in silence while I read about beheadings and disembowelings, about corpses left in pieces all over property, about candles and black magic and pagan ceremonies.

In each, the bodies remained.

"You don't think they did it," I said, as I tossed my sandwich wrapper into the nearby trash.

"The cult?" He shook his head. "No, I don't think so."

"But the evidence points to them."

"Rather neatly," he said.

"So why didn't you speak up?"

"Because I had no other theory of the case," he said.

"Do you now?" I asked.

"Does your friend work for the catering firm?" And I realized he meant the man with the angular face.

"I think so."

"I'll see if I can track him down."

"And if you do?"

Foreno shrugged. "I'll see what happens next."

***

I WENT BACK TO WORK, thinking about all that blood, all those trails. The carpets were saturated, yet there were no footprints on the hardwood floors, no evidence of someone leaving through the front or back doors. The floors had been well-scrubbed with bleach, and one of the things I testified about was the way that bleach hid all evidence, one of the few things that masked even the goriest scene.

Why, the defense attorney had wanted to know, *would someone remove the footprints, but leave the blood droplets? Why leave the drag marks on the carpet uncleaned?*

I had shrugged. *People aren't that thorough. They clean only what they believe needs cleaning.*

Blood is blood, isn't it? he had asked, implying that someone who cleaned footprints on the hardwood would clean it all.

It's not that simple, I said. *I've had employees who missed spatter on their first few jobs because the scene was too overwhelming.*

Do you think the killer would be overwhelmed? The defense attorney had asked, but the prosecutor had objected to the question. I never got to answer.

Would the killer have been overwhelmed? I considered the question now, at the safety of my desk. Probably not. After all, he created the scene.

Three saturated carpets. Five dead humans. Six quarts of blood per body. That house was soaked, the scene an example—the prosecutor had said—of overkill.

We see what we want to see.

I went back to my notes and, for the first time, did the math.

***

THERE WAS TOO MUCH BLOOD. None of us had realized it. At least twice the amount that should have been in that house. Twice the deaths? Or had someone taken buckets of blood and poured it on the carpets, letting the liquid soak in after he had expertly sprayed the walls.

Reproducing crime scenes wasn't hard. Hollywood did it all the time, and there were photos of other scenes everywhere from forensic journals to true crime novels. Spatter and spray would be easy to reproduce—plant misters, set just right, would mimic the early parts of spray, and something with a bit of kick would be able to reproduce the way that blood spurted from an artery.

There'd be mistakes, but who would look for them? Especially in an overwhelming and fairly obvious scene.

Too much blood wasn't enough for Foreno to reopen the case—it was a closed murder trial, after all. But the blood evidence, coupled with the young man I'd seen, was enough to get Foreno working it again, on the side, in his spare time.

First, he had a crime scene friend re-examine the photos, not explaining anything about the case.

Second, he looked in the Moorhead family background.

Third, he searched for the waiter.

And those three things came together into something both expected and unexpected. The tech said the scene might've been tampered with. Impossible to know now, although the blood was suspicious. Maybe someone else died.

The Moorheads traveled. They were running from debt in Michigan and used charm as well as the co-signature of an old friend to secure the house, which then got them credit cards and a new future.

Until the bank was ready to foreclose. Until the credit card companies had cut them off.

And the co-signer? The same man who had waited tables that night. The one who had overseen the court case. He was living under an alias, one he'd established twenty years before after he had embezzled fifty thousand dollars from a bank in the Midwest.

The bank where his brother had once worked.

The waiter wouldn't talk to the police—hiring a lawyer immediately—but his presence was enough to get those carpet samples tested.

Still refrigerated, still intact after all these years. Sometimes laziness was its own reward.

And that, Foreno said when he came to my office in May, was when it got interesting. The blood was all the same type—O Positive—but that was all it had in common. DNA testing proved that the blood came from dozens of sources, none of them related to the so-called victims.

Just the blood on the wall came from the family and, judging by the overlap in one of the bedrooms, had been applied just like I mentioned, with a sprayer and a lot of determination.

"Why?" I asked. "Why not just disappear? These people were smart enough to create new identities once before."

And that was when he showed me the police files. He'd actually made copies for me so that I could look at them.

Pages and pages and pages of complaints filed by the family, about the neighbors, about the young people in the house at the foot of the hill, about the parties and the goings-on, about the fears of devil worship and a possible cult.

Foreno shook his head. "Looks to me like pure old-fashioned hatred."

"For their neighbors?"

"Their young, unusual, and loud neighbors," Foreno said.

"They set these kids up?" I asked, and felt a shock at myself. I was willing to believe that a cult could off an entire family; I was not willing to believe that a family would set up innocent people in a way that might send them to jail for life.

"Looks like it," he said. "We've got work to do. They've got ten years and a lot of thinking on us."

"But you'll find them," I said.

"I hope so," he said. "But in life, there are no guarantees."

***

EXCEPT ONE.

The story leaked, and the leak coincided with the release of the annual budget. The party, the plans for the museum, and the cost to the taxpayer made page one of our usually sleepy rag.

For a while, it looked like Louise might implode because of the scandal. Then she hit on the right note: the case wouldn't be reopened—innocent people wouldn't be getting out of jail—if she hadn't been interested in the house in the first place.

She had a point, one I didn't care to think about.

Then one afternoon shortly after Halloween, I had to go to the Moorhead House for the final time.

***

I went with various attorneys—the D.A., several assistants, and defense attorneys for a variety of clients from the waiter to the cult. Someone had found the youngest son in Miami, but he hadn't given up the rest of his family. His very presence—alive—in another state was enough to place doubt on the entire cult-killings story.

He wasn't represented by an attorney, so far as I knew, but I didn't ask a lot of questions.

Instead, I answered them, explaining what chemicals I used, defending myself and why I hadn't noticed the irregularities in the spatter, the extra blood, the lack of footprints.

Over and over again, I said simply that it wasn't my job.

And it wasn't. I was supposed to clean, not think. I was supposed to make the place livable again, and I had.

I had done everything I'd contracted to do.

Maybe that was why the house had haunted me so. Why I had dreamed of it, why the blood kept reappearing on the walls—not as if it couldn't be buried, but as if there was too much of it to contain.

My subconscious had known.

My conscious had refused to accept anything but what it had been told: a family had been murdered by their neighbors, a murderous cult, and the bodies hidden.

Differing interpretations of the same evidence—evidence not examined closely by any of us.

Except the brother, who had made two mistakes. First, he had come to the trial—nervously and obsessively worrying—to see if anyone had found the planted evidence. Or maybe he was stunned and appalled that a case with no bodies generated enough evidence for a conviction. Maybe the family had merely meant to harass the cult, not destroy their lives.

Then he had come back to the house, deliberately getting hired, just so he could see the site of his—and his family's—triumph. Or maybe he had still been worried, still afraid that he would get caught. Maybe he was guarding the place, hoping that no one figured it out.

Or maybe he simply couldn't stay away.

Like I couldn't.

I take evidence of a hideous event and make it vanish. I call that healing, but really, it's just masking. The event remains. It is history; it has happened. I allow people to pretend everything is all right.

What happened in the Moorhead House that day was the opposite of what I do. That family had used a masking technique to get revenge on people they hated, and in the process, managed to disappear with no consequences at all. They left debts, and dozens of families in ruins.

They left a chair pushed out, and knew that we would assume the worst.

We prosecuted based on that assumption, and received a conviction. And I cleaned up the mess so thoroughly that we have to use photographs and cut pieces of rug, miraculously saved. We can't revisit the scene with Luminol, trying to see what had happened before, because I had smeared it, trying to make the home safe, trying to make it—and us—forget.

We'll never know for certain what happened in that house. Just like we'll never know why another neighbor down the street finished his pie last Thanksgiving and then took his own life.

Just like I'll never know how long my mother lay on the floor of her kitchen, conscious and hoping someone would find her.

We can clean the mess, but the uncertainties remain.

There are Christmas lights around the Moorhead House this year, but there will be no party. It's not in the budget. Once the appeals are over, once the trials have ended, the house will become a museum, just like Louise dreamed.

But people aren't going to go inside to look at one of the city's first houses, thinking about old Josiah Moorhead and the power he had because he had the foresight to build ferries that crossed the river. People will go into his house to see if they can find that one piece of evidence, that one spot of blood, that one thing I might have missed in my thorough cleaning, hoping to see if they can solve the case that nearly cost a group of rowdy and unconventional young people their lives.

I won't go back. I'm not going into any damaged houses any more. I'm strictly management now—assigning teams, paying bills. I can't look at interiors filled with the leftovers of other people's lives, and worry that something important has been missed.

I don't want that responsibility.

My imagination is too strong, my memories too fresh.

I don't need any more ghosts.

I have enough already.

About the Author

INTERNATIONAL BESTSELLING WRITER Kristine Kathryn Rusch has lived in Oregon since 1986. She has published fiction in every genre. She has been nominated for awards in all those genres as well. She is best known for her science fiction and fantasy, although her mainstream novel *Hitler's Angel,* recently appeared in the United Kingdom to great critical acclaim. She has also published award-winning mystery novels under the name Kris Nelscott. For more about her work, go to kristinekathrynrusch.com.

Also by
Kristine Kathryn Rusch

The Retrieval Artist Series:

The Disappeared
Extremes
Consequences
Buried Deep
Paloma
Recovery Man
Duplicate Effort
Anniversary Day
Blowback

The Smokey Dalton Series (as Kris Nelscott):

A Dangerous Road
Smoke-Filled Rooms
Thin Walls
Stone Cribs
War at Home
Days of Rage

wMG
Publishing